CS

Their reun
sweet and s
face with kis
r

Eve had never experienced such wonderful
kisses. Feverish kisses of relief. Kisses of two souls
seeking a fulfillment beyond just the physical.

"I was terrified they'd caught up with you," she
said. "That you were dead."

"Would I do that to you? Never. I managed to
outrun them."

"Where—" Eve sucked in her breath as his
mouth traveled to her jaw, then her cheeks. She
exhaled slowly, weakly. "Where are they now, do
you suppose?"

"Gave up for the night, I imagine, and returned
to their chopper. What else could they do?"

His lips had found her eyes, which she'd closed
to accommodate him. He tenderly kissed each
lid. Trembling, she croaked, "But they'll be back,
won't they? They won't quit."

"Yeah, sooner or later they'll be back."

★ ★ ★

Dear Reader,

Is there any chance that, like me, you just can't get enough stories about two people on the run from danger? I sure hope so, because that's what I'm giving you in *AWOL with the Operative*. Of course, a story like this isn't any good without a highly sensual romance. And although there are always the obstacles of a deadly enemy in pursuit to be overcome, there must also be the personal conflicts between hero and heroine that have to be resolved before they can earn that happily-ever-after they deserve.

There is another important ingredient in such stories—the setting. In the case of *AWOL with the Operative*, the setting is the frozen Canadian wilderness, where Eve and Sam have to deal with the enemy and learn how to survive in a hostile environment. Now that's a challenge in itself. Are you up to it?

Jean Thomas

JEAN THOMAS

AWOL with the Operative

ROMANTIC
SUSPENSE

Recycling programs
for this product may
not exist in your area.

ISBN-13: 978-0-373-27764-3

AWOL WITH THE OPERATIVE

This edition published by arrangement with Harlequin Books S.A.

For questions and comments about the quality of this book
please contact us at Customer_eCare@Harlequin.ca.

® and TM are trademarks of Harlequin Books S.A., used under license.
Trademarks indicated with ® are registered in the United States Patent
and Trademark Office, the Canadian Trade Marks Office and in other
countries.

www.Harlequin.com

Printed in U.S.A.

Books by Jean Thomas

Harlequin Romantic Suspense
AWOL with the Operative #1694

JEAN THOMAS

aka Jean Barrett, lives in Wisconsin in an English-style cottage on a Lake Michigan store bluff. The view from her office window would be a magnificent one if it weren't blocked by a big fat computer that keeps demanding her attention.

The author of twenty-four romances was a teacher before she left the classroom to write full-time. A longtime member of Romance Writers of America, Jean is the proud winner of three national awards and has appeared on several bestseller lists. When she isn't at the keyboard, she likes to take long walks that churn up new story ideas or work in the garden, which never seems to churn up anything but dirt. Of course, there are always books to be read. Romantic suspenses are her favorite. No surprise there.

To Betty Straus. Thank you, Betty, for your loyal readership through the years. It is deeply appreciated.

Chapter 1

The first thing Sam noticed about her was the fear in her eyes.

Okay, maybe not the first. If he was going to be honest with himself, the first had to be how tantalizing those eyes were. That is, if a pair of eyes could be described as tantalizing. Hers could, he decided. Definitely. They were wide, framed by dark lashes and a pure, luminous green.

But, yeah, at the moment registering her fear. Understandable, he supposed, considering how her boyfriend had died. And now she was at risk herself. Or so Sam's squad supervisor believed. Sam, himself, had yet to be convinced of that.

"Anything new on the case?" he asked the ruddy-faced RCMP officer, to whom he had just presented his American passport and his FBI credentials.

The young Mountie, standing protectively at Eve Warren's side, shook his head. "We're still investigating. That particular stretch of road can be real bad, especially in winter conditions. Either the accident was just that, an accident, or—"

The Mountie glanced at Eve, plainly not wanting her to hear the rest. But Sam could guess what he must have intended to say.

Or Charlie Fowler's rental car was forced off the road and down that mountainside where he fell to his death.

"It was snowing, you see," the Mountie explained, "and the tire tracks were no longer visible for us to read. But a witness on the lower road thought there was another car up there behind Fowler's. If so, it disappeared from the scene."

Sam gazed at Eve. If she was upset listening to what she must have heard already, it wasn't visible on her face. Except for the fear that was still in her eyes. Other than that, she was silent. Just as she had been since Sam had introduced himself a moment ago when he had arrived in the lobby of the main lodge. They had been waiting for him.

Could be she was in a state of shock. Damn. He was in no mood to deal with anything like that. This situation was bad enough as it was.

The Mountie returned Sam's wallet folder containing his picture ID and badge, which he tucked back into his coat pocket, along with his passport. "Unless there's anything else, Special Agent McDonough, I'll turn Miss Warren over to you."

Sam nodded and addressed himself to Eve with a brusque, "You ready?"

"Yes."

Her voice was low and husky. And every bit as sexy

as her green eyes, Sam thought. One more thing he was in no mood to deal with.

They both started to reach for her suitcase at the same time. Their fingers made contact. Sam swore he felt a jolt of current that was decidedly not static electricity shoot clear up his arm—something he was determined to ignore. She must have felt it, too. She quickly withdrew her hand, letting him take possession of her suitcase.

Eve thanked the Mountie for guarding her and accompanied Sam out the front door and down the steps to his waiting rental car. He stowed her bag in the trunk and saw her settled in the passenger seat. Then, before climbing behind the wheel, he did a fast check of the area to be sure it was secure. They were alone.

God, what a place for a high-class skiing village, he thought as he started the car and headed away from the lodge. April, and still as cold and white as mid-January. He supposed that was the point, to be located somewhere that would extend the season as long as possible. Yeah, but did it have to be in the Yukon wilderness, remote and isolated? Perfect for Charlie Fowler, though. A safe spot for his little tryst with Eve Warren. Or so Charlie must have believed.

The driveway out to the main road took them winding through the village's colony of chalets. The chalets were presumably occupied by guests who preferred the small, Swiss-style structures over accommodations in the lodge.

"You and Fowler stay in one of those or in the lodge?" Sam asked the woman beside him.

"In a chalet," Eve informed him. She didn't point out which one.

Figures it would be a chalet, Sam thought. More privacy that way. And Charlie Fowler would have wanted as much privacy with her as possible. The FBI special agent would bet they never wasted a moment out on the ski slopes.

Sam didn't blame Fowler. If he'd been holed up with a woman like Eve Warren, he'd want her all to himself, too. Or he would have before his life went all to hell. Now it was just a question of getting through each day without losing his sanity.

They had reached the main road. Sam turned right. When Eve realized which direction they were headed in, she challenged him with a startled "This isn't the way to Dawson!"

"We're not going to the commercial airport in Dawson."

"Stop the car and turn around!"

Sam stopped the car. "Yeah, we can do that," he said, not bothering to soften the sarcasm in his tone. "We can turn around and head for Dawson. That what you really want? To climb up over that pass where Charlie died?"

She didn't respond, but when he turned his head to look at her, he saw her shudder with something like grief or dread. Maybe both.

"I didn't think so," he said without offering any sympathy as he drove on.

"Then where *are* you taking us?"

"To a small airfield used by private planes. I've arranged for us to be flown out of here by one of the bush pilots there. Any more questions?"

He shouldn't have given her the opportunity. Should have known she'd have one. The woman was turning out to be a real pain in the ass.

"But why?"

"Because I'm a cautious agent, Eve Warren. If Fowler *was* murdered, then whoever killed him could be watching either that road or the airport in Dawson, just waiting for you to turn up. Okay?"

She must have been satisfied with his explanation because she offered no more objections. Not that he would tolerate them if she did. All that mattered to him was that she obey his instructions. The sooner he got her to Chicago and turned her over to his boss, the sooner he could walk away and get back to his life. What remained of it, that is.

He could see she was nervous, though. Her body went rigid every time they encountered an icy patch on the road, with the car starting to slide sideways before he corrected it.

Although he periodically checked the rearview mirror to make certain they weren't being followed, there was no other vehicle either in front or behind them. They were on their own out here.

When he wasn't concentrating on the road, Sam found himself sneaking glances at the woman beside him. Not wise. Not wise at all, but he couldn't seem to help himself.

She was an eyeful all right. A mass of russet-colored hair, creamy complexion, a beguiling little cleft in her chin and a full mouth that…well, a mouth that could only be described as lush.

He couldn't see her body under that bulky parka, but he was willing to imagine it was every bit as alluring as the rest of her. And that made him even more puzzled about her than he'd been back in Chicago.

"What was this Eve Warren doing up there with Fowler?" Sam had asked his squad supervisor. "According to the record you have on him, he was never married, so she couldn't have been his wife. There wasn't a mention of any ongoing affair, either. So just who is she?"

Frank Kowsloski, hands folded across his paunch as he rocked back in his desk chair, had just shrugged. "We don't know. We didn't even know she existed until the RCMP called us with the news of Fowler's death. And since then…well, there's been no time for any proper investigation. All we could learn were the basics online. Her address, that she's single, parents deceased, works for a magazine in St. Louis. That kind of thing."

"Seems to me Fowler could have told you he was meeting someone up there." Sam hadn't been able to keep the sour note out of his voice as he'd faced Frank across his littered desktop. He'd resented being called in like this. Still did.

"Look, I was lucky to even persuade him in the end to tell us where he was going. I could have lost him if I'd pushed too hard."

And that, Sam had thought, would have meant losing the FBI's prime opportunity to send one of the nation's most notorious crime bosses to prison. Because Charlie Fowler had been Victor DeMarco's longtime accountant. He'd had the evidence to convict DeMarco, records that would prove years of tax cheating. And Charlie had been willing to turn those records over to the FBI. Why? Terminal cancer. Apparently, Charlie had also suffered from an attack of conscience and a need to make things right before he died.

But now it was too late. For all his careful handling of the case, Frank had lost Charlie Fowler anyway on that road to Dawson.

"Why didn't you send an agent up there with him?" Sam had pressed his boss.

Frank had shaken his head. "He anticipated that. Said if one of my agents turned up there, the whole deal was off. Guess he wanted this last fling of his, if that's what it was, to be strictly private. Anyway, the Canadians don't appreciate our agents operating up there, not without permission and a lot of red tape. I had to settle for the Mounties promising to keep an eye on him."

Which hadn't worked, Sam thought, although he knew the RCMP was a reliable law enforcement agency.

"Why me, Frank? Why do I get to be your delivery boy? Hell, you know I'm not ready to come off leave. I'm still a head case."

"Can't be helped, Sam. All our agents are either out in the field or off somewhere with their kids on their spring vacations. Disney World, for all I know."

Yeah, Sam had thought, *warm* places. Not the freeze-your-ass-off Yukon Territory. Why had Charlie Fowler chosen such a spot? Probably because he'd figured it was absolutely safe. It hadn't been, not if he was murdered because DeMarco had suspected his accountant was about to turn on him. If that was true, it meant DeMarco's boys had somehow managed to find him.

"You know, Frank, it would have been a helluva lot easier if Fowler had just turned those records over to you before he took off for the Yukon."

"But he wouldn't, not until his return. Probably his way of making sure I'd stick to my end of the bargain. I had no choice but to play by his rules." The squad supervisor had hunched forward in his chair with an earnest "Look, it's a simple enough assignment. All you have to do is fly up there and bring Eve Warren out. I need her, Sam. My gut tells me if DeMarco's goons haven't managed to get their hands on those records, then the woman either has them or knows where they are."

Sam had doubted that then in Frank's office, and he doubted it now even more after meeting Eve Warren. There was nothing about her to indicate that Fowler would have trusted her with such important information. No, given her spectacular looks and the considerable age difference between Fowler and her, Sam would wager she had to be nothing more than a playmate hired by Charlie to share his last holiday.

But, yeah, Sam could understand all right why Fowler had wanted her. Temptation that she was, he desired her himself. Not that he would try to initiate anything. She was his assignment, and that was all. Period.

Still, Charlie Fowler must have cared for her on some level other than a purely carnal one. The report Sam had read on his flight up here indicated Charlie and Eve had flown separately to Dawson and that Fowler had intended them to return in the same manner, which was why Eve wasn't in that rental car with him. Why had Charlie insisted on that? Because he had wanted to safeguard her in the event of trouble? Sam wondered...

She didn't like him.

On a purely physical level, Eve thought, Sam McDonough might qualify as every woman's ideal male fantasy. He certainly had all the right, rugged looks for it. She wouldn't deny him that.

All right, so in that sense she wasn't entirely immune to him herself. But his attitude...well, that was another matter. The man was a devil—nasty to the point of harshness.

If he had any sympathy for her loss, he didn't bother to express it either by word or manner. One thing was clear. He resented her.

Eve didn't bother to wonder why. She was suffering from too much grief over Charlie's death to trouble herself with something that didn't really matter.

Charlie, Charlie, what happened exactly? And why did it have to happen?

She missed him. Missed him terribly. She was alone now. Alone and frightened.

Not quite alone, Eve. There's the man at your side. But why, oh why, do you have to be so aware of him and this very disturbing effect he has on you?

It was impossible to ignore him as she would have liked. He was too blatantly there. Very much of a forceful presence with his hard body and hot temper.

An FBI agent of all things. They had sent an FBI agent to escort her home. Something connected with Charlie, and she was clear about none of it. Still too traumatized by the whole thing to try to figure it out. Or could it be that she didn't really want to know?

How had she managed to get herself into this terrible situation anyway? She was just an ordinary girl living an ordinary life. Work, a nice apartment, good friends, occasional dates when both her mood and interest prompted her enough to go out with the men who asked her.

Pleasant company. None of them that held the promise of anything approaching a serious attachment. None of them any more extraordinary than she was. No secrets in her life, no suggestion of intrigue. And no man who assaulted her senses while managing to be hateful about it at the same time. Until now.

The airfield was a simple one—two runways recently plowed for takeoffs and landings and a metal hangar attached to a small building that must serve as an office.

Their pilot emerged from the structure, shaking hands with them when Sam and Eve climbed out of the car. He was a portly, middle-aged man with the look of a

Native American. Or at least a mixture of ancestry, Sam thought.

The guy verified that when he introduced himself. "Ken Redfeather," he said. "Plane's all gassed and ready for you."

Sam nodded in the direction of the rental car. "There'll be someone who'll return the car to the Dawson airport, won't there?"

"Yep. All arranged for, just as you specified on the phone. This way, folks."

Ken Redfeather led them out to the waiting plane, a single engine, high-wing craft. Insisting on carrying her own suitcase this time, Eve followed their pilot. Sam brought up the rear with his own bag.

Why the hell couldn't he keep his eyes off her? First it was her face. Now it was her backside. Or, anyway, what he could see of it in that coat. Whether the seductive sway of her hips was done consciously or unconsciously, whether it was fair of him or not, he resented her for his arousal. Emotionally messed up as he was, he didn't need this unexpected complication.

Redfeather took their luggage when they reached the plane and stowed it in a baggage compartment behind the seats. Apparently a conscientious pilot, he invited them to settle themselves inside while he checked the outside of the plane to make sure everything was sound.

Ducking under the wing, Sam folded the front passenger seat back. "You take the backseat," he indicated to Eve.

"Why?"

"Because there are no windows back there to speak of. You'll be more secure."

"And just what do you think I could possibly be in danger from up there? Birds?"

"It's not birds I'm worried about. I don't want you being a possible visible target when we land for refueling, which I was told when I made the arrangements that we'd have to do before we set down in Calgary."

"And after Calgary?"

"We board a commercial jet for Chicago. No more questions. Get in the back."

"I don't think so," she said stubbornly. "It's bound to be warmer in front near the heater."

"So, just keep your coat on."

"I'd still like to ride in front."

"I'm not giving you that choice," he informed her sharply. "Just do what I tell you when I tell you, and we'll both be happy."

He could tell by the way her eyebrows lifted and the ice-hard glare under them that she was royally pissed off with him. Well, that was her problem.

"Has anyone ever told you that you're rude to the point of—"

"Meanness? Yeah, plenty of times. So what?"

She muttered something under her breath that he didn't catch. He could guess what it might be. Something that probably involved the word *bastard*. Too bad. She had to understand he was responsible for her. That meant, like it or not—and she obviously didn't anymore than he did—following his instructions.

"I'm beginning to think the only threat to me is you, Special Agent McDonough."

One of those shapely eyebrows of hers, which Sam was beginning to realize were capable of expressing a whole range of emotions, shot up again with barely restrained anger. Before she could go on arguing with him, he cut her off with an emphatic, "Now get in the back like a good girl, and try not to give me any more grief."

She must have figured it wasn't worth the effort to make a further issue of it. Long-strapped, leather purse swinging from her shoulder, she clambered aboard and into the backseat. Sam lowered the front seat and swung himself into it. He shut the door behind him as Ken Redfeather rounded the tail of the plane and approached the pilot's door.

As cramped as the cabin was, Sam wondered how Redfeather, with that ample belly of his, could possibly fit behind the yoke. As it turned out, once he'd shed his coat, he managed it with relative ease.

"Belt up, folks, and we'll get my girl here on her way."

A few minutes later, the plane lifted off the runway and into the clear, blue sky. When they had reached their cruising altitude, Sam looked down over the side.

The terrain spread out below them was an impressive sight. Snowy mountains, frozen lakes, vast forests of white spruce, birch and fir. On the flat, treeless bowl of a valley, Sam thought he could spot what had to be a herd of elk.

"Beautiful, isn't it?" Redfeather said, obviously proud of his rugged homeland.

Sam murmured his agreement. Eve, probably unable to catch more than glimpses of what lay below them, had nothing to contribute. Sam should have felt some guilt about that and didn't. Hey, he was only ensuring her welfare, wasn't he?

Needing to confirm that welfare after a long silence in the cabin, he twisted around in his seat to check on her. And learned she was waiting for him. Or so it seemed when their gazes collided head-on. Sam sucked in his breath as her green, siren's eyes held his, searing him with a hot intensity.

The moment was a compelling one. He had never felt

so inflamed by a woman. And he didn't appreciate it. Not when his self-control was in jeopardy by this senseless attraction to a woman he'd met less than two hours before. Not when he felt helpless to do anything about it, except damn himself for a weakness he couldn't afford.

She finally broke the contact, dragging her gaze away from his, her face flushed. That's when Sam realized she was not only conscious of him on the same level but that she didn't want this tug of strong emotions between them any more than he did.

Releasing his breath with a rush of air, he turned around in his seat to avoid the provocative sight of her. Ken Redfeather appeared to be unmindful of the whole exchange. Sam meant to keep it that way.

"Think I'll catch a few winks," Sam mumbled. "I didn't have a chance to sleep on the flight up here."

Focused on his flying, Redfeather merely nodded.

It was warm up front, probably why Redfeather had wisely rid himself of his coat before takeoff. Something else that Sam should have felt guilty about, especially since he meant to follow the pilot's example. Unbuckling his seat belt, he squirmed out of his own coat and dropped it down beside Redfeather's in the space between them.

Sam restored his belt before he slid down in the seat as much as his tall body would allow. He closed his eyes, but, although he needed the rest, he didn't expect to sleep. He didn't sleep much at all these days, not even in his own bed. And with Eve Warren very much on his mind...

Sam must have dozed off after all. For how long he had no idea. The next thing he knew, the pilot was calling to him.

"Agent McDonough, wake up! I need you!"

Sam didn't like the insistent, concerned tone in Redfeather's voice. Shaking off the fog of sleep in his head, he sat up on his seat, instantly alert.

"What is it? Something wrong?"

"I hope not. *That* out there has been tailing us."

The pilot nodded in the direction of the window on his side. Sam leaned over to get a better view through the glass. *That* proved to be a sizable helicopter of the military variety.

"How long has it been out there?"

"Not sure. But it has to be a powerful chopper to keep up with us."

Not only keep up with them, Sam realized, but overtake them. The craft was flying level now with their plane a few hundred yards straight off to their left.

"Maybe it's an official chopper patrolling the region. Just checking us out to make sure we're legitimate."

Ken Redfeather shook his head. "I don't think so, not in this area. Anyway, I've never seen anything like it before."

"What's happening?" Eve demanded to know.

Sam had forgotten that, except for a very small pane on either side, she had no window back there. He turned his head to make sure she was all right. "Probably nothing. Just keep low until we know," he ordered her curtly. He swung his attention back to their pilot. "Can you rouse them on your radio? Ask them what they're doing out there?"

"I can try."

Before Redfeather could act, the helicopter suddenly and rapidly closed the gap between them until it was no more than a couple of hundred feet away. A door in the side of the craft rolled back, revealing a burly, bearded man kneeling there in the opening with a rifle raised to his shoulder. Within seconds, Sam could hear bullets pinging against the body of their plane.

Sonofabitch!

"They're shooting at us!" Redfeather shouted.

Sam concurred with a caustic "I noticed that."

He knew what their objective was. Eve Warren. He also knew who they were. Had to be Victor DeMarco's goons ordered to bring their plane down. But how in hell had they learned his method of transport?

No time to worry about that. Somehow he had to get them out of this mess, but first—

"You okay?" he asked, whipping his head around. "You weren't hit, were—?"

He broke off in exasperation. Although she managed to shake her head, she went on sitting there upright, looking too numb with terror to move.

"Didn't I tell you to get down?"

"Stop bullying me!"

"Then, dammit, do as you're told."

The look of alarm on her face was joined now by rancor directed at him. But she complied this time, squeezing down as low as possible in her seat.

Satisfied, Sam faced forward again, snatching his Glock out of his shoulder holster. Not that it would be of much use at this distance against a powerful rifle, but he felt better with the gun in his grip. He scanned the sky out his window. Not a cloud in sight. Wait a minute. There, below them!

"We've got cloud cover under us," he informed Redfeather. "Looks big enough to hide in."

"It's a low snow mass."

"Man, I don't care if it's a typhoon. Just get us into it, and fast."

Ken Redfeather obeyed him, pushing the yoke forward. The nose of the plane went down, sending them into a dive. Sam steadied himself against the plunge, hoping Eve was hanging on. And hoping even more that Redfeather had the skill to get them out of this steep descent once they were buried in the cloud mass.

If the helicopter was swooping after them, Sam had no indication of it. At least there was no further gunfire from the chopper. None that he could detect anyway.

Small comfort, Sam thought wryly, remembering his squad supervisor's certainty. It looked like Frank Kowsloski had been right about Eve Warren. That she did know something vital enough for Victor DeMarco to want her taken down. In this case, *literally.*

So much for a simple pickup and delivery. Squad supervisor or not, he was going to blister Frank when he got back. *If* he got back.

A fog closed in on the plane, cloaking them with its thickness. Snowflakes swirled around them, adding to their cover. They were in the cloud mass.

To Sam's relief, Ken Redfeather pulled them out of the dive. They were flying level again. He searched through the windows on both sides. No sign of the chopper. They were safe. At least for the moment.

"Where are we anyway?" he wanted to know.

"On the border between British Columbia and Alberta," Redfeather said.

"Not anywhere near Calgary, I suppose, since we haven't stopped for refueling."

"No, Calgary is still a long way off."

Sam checked on Eve. "You holding up?"

"Just dandy," she answered him dryly.

He guessed that was all the reassurance he was going to get. He wasn't going to ask for more. He'd had enough of her obstinate crap. Besides, he had another concern to address. He switched his attention back to Redfeather.

"I don't know about you, Ken, but I think it's time you got on your radio and called out a distress. Let them know what's happening up here."

"I'll try, but I'm not sure I'm in range of one of the towers. Bush pilots have been complaining for years about the dead zones out here." Redfeather reached for his mike. "Let's see if I can reach—" He broke off, staring in alarm down at the instrument panel.

"What is it? What's wrong?"

"The oil pressure is dropping—and dropping fast. One of those bullets must have struck a push rod tube, and now we're leaking oil at the bottom of the cowling."

Great. Another freaking complication. "How bad is that?"

"Real bad. You want it straight?"

"Let's have it."

"Without oil, the engine will lock up and quit. I'm surprised she hasn't already—"

There was a sudden, sickly sputtering. It was happening. The engine was seizing up. Sam heard a horrified gasp from the rear seat, and then there was nothing but a terrible stillness. The engine was dead.

The plane drifted for a few seconds, and then Sam could feel it settling as it lost altitude on its descent through the cloud cover.

"I'll try to glide us in for a safe landing, folks, but it'll be a miracle if there's a clearing down there. Better make sure your belts are tight before you fold yourselves into a crash position."

Sam whirled around in his seat, barking a command at Eve. "Brace yourself! Head on your knees!"

But she knew the drill. Her head was already lowered,

face hidden against her knees. Sam risked a quick glance through the window. They had broken through the cloud mass. The ground was coming up on them swiftly. There was nothing down there resembling a clearing, only the dense, unbroken forest.

Sam ducked down, straining against his belt to get his head on his knees. A few seconds later, they plowed into the forest. He could hear the undercarriage tearing apart as the plane, nose down, smashed through the limbs of the trees.

The action jerked him up, slamming his head against the window on his side. He felt a sharp, shooting pain, and then everything went black.

Chapter 2

For a full moment after the plane came to rest Eve was too shaken to move. Then slowly, carefully, she lifted her head from her knees. Dazed. She was so dazed she was imagining she was tipped over at a crazy angle. That had to be the explanation.

It was only when she struggled to sit up on the seat that she realized she *was* at a crazy angle. Or at least the plane was.

But as rough as the impact of crashing into the forest was, it had been softened somewhat by all the branches that had snatched at them on the way down. Must be the reason why, when she tested her own limbs, they seemed to work just fine. No other injuries she was aware of, either.

Shaking her head to clear it, Eve tried to see through the thick gloom of the cabin. It was hard to distinguish anything in the dim light of the forest and with the broken boughs of the evergreens plastered against the shattered windows on all sides.

She became conscious then of something else in the cabin. The awful silence. Sam McDonough, the pilot! Why wasn't she hearing them? Why weren't they stirring?

For another long, stunned moment she was too fearful of the answer to move. But she couldn't go on sitting here like this. She had to *know,* had to help them. If it wasn't too late. But she wouldn't let herself believe that it was.

She made an effort to get to her feet, and couldn't. The seat belt, of course. She was still tightly restrained by it. Her fingers were unsteady, but she managed to unbuckle the belt and stagger to her feet. With her sight adjusted now to the murky light, she immediately learned the worst when, supporting herself against the tilt of the plane, she leaned over the back of the pilot's seat.

Ken Redfeather's head was at an unnatural angle. The kind of angle that said his neck was broken. His eyes were open. And sightless. There was no question of it. The man was dead. Had Charlie looked like this after his own death? The possibility was so unbearable that Eve thrust the image out of her mind.

She willed herself not to start wailing in shock and sorrow. Sam McDonough needed her attention. She moved on to him. He was slumped against the passenger door. Cracks radiated in the glass of the window where his head rested, an indication he must have suffered a severe blow when his head struck the window.

No evidence of any blood, but she could detect a sizable lump already swelling on the side of his head. She prayed he was still alive.

His collar was open at his throat. Searching for a pulse, her hand brushed against the stubble on his jaw.

She tried not to think how warm his skin was, how touching him like this felt both wrong and right at the same time.

Stop it. There's nothing wrong or right about it. It's simply a necessity in a bad situation.

To her relief, she located a pulse in his neck. It was strong and even—a confirmation that he was unconscious and not dead. But maybe injured internally, perhaps with a concussion, and needing medical care.

What should she do? What *could* she do?

There was the radio. Call out a Mayday? Impossible. Even if the radio was still working, she had no idea how to operate it. Besides, Ken Redfeather had said it was unreliable in the air and down here in the forest…

Eve had never felt so helpless, so close to outright panic. She gazed wildly around the tight cabin, as if looking for a miracle. There was no miracle. There was only another serious discovery. Through the window on the pilot's side, she could see gas dripping down from the crumpled wing. And she could smell it through a gap in the glass. There was something else she could smell. Smoke!

Dear God, the plane must be on fire somewhere, and if the flames reached those wings where the fuel was stored—

You can't go on standing here doing nothing.

She had to act, had to get both Sam and herself out of the plane before it went up like a firestorm. The door on the pilot's side provided no exit. It was blocked by a heavy tree limb. It would have to be the passenger door.

Summoning what she hoped was a sufficient measure of strength and fortitude, Eve leaned over Sam as far as she could. It wasn't easy getting a grip on those shoulders of his, not when they were so wide and hard as stone. But she somehow managed to lever him away from the door in slow degrees and finally to heave him over to the left.

She was puffing from exertion by then. Although the door latch was exposed now, she had to pause long enough to catch her breath. She used the opportunity to check on the fire. She could see the source of it now through the cracked windshield. Little wisps of smoke were curling up from the nose where the engine was located. No visible flames yet, but if she didn't hurry—

Eve took up the battle again, straining to reach the latch. No good. The only way she could get at it was from the front. There was a narrow gap between the door and the passenger seat. Wedging herself in the opening, body twisting and squirming, she managed to squeeze through. The awkward effort cost her her balance, almost landing her in Sam's lap.

Righting herself, she attacked the latch. The door was stuck. What if she couldn't get it open? What if they were trapped in here?

She refused to accept that. This time she put her shoulder to it, shoving ferociously with an equally fierce curse of frustration. "Open up, damn you!"

The door popped wide with a suddenness that almost pitched her out into the snow. Recovering herself again, she realized that her purse was getting in the way, hindering her every move as it swayed like a pendulum from her shoulder. She tossed the bag out on the ground.

The action reminded her that she had to free Sam of his seat belt. Twisting herself around, she groped for the catch on the belt. Her fumbling fingers couldn't avoid coming in contact with his waist. Again she experienced that sensation of firm, warm flesh, of something intimate and forbidden just beneath the fabric of his shirt. It was a giddy pleasure that made her want to—

The catch snapped open, releasing Sam. Backing quickly away from him, Eve lowered herself to the ground, leaned into the opening and caught him by the ankles.

This part isn't going to be easy.

And it wasn't. However, gravity was on her side this time. The crooked plane was tipped to the right, making her effort all downhill. With a combination of tugging and sheer force of will, she eased him out over the side where she was finally able to drop him into the snow.

What he might have suffered in the process, Eve didn't allow herself to imagine. Her struggle wasn't done. Raising his arms over his head and gripping him by his big hands, she dragged him inch by inch away from the plane. He was a heavy, solid man, but the snow helped, letting her slide his body over its slick surface.

Eve delivered him a safe distance away from the hazardous plane. Winded, she wanted nothing more than to collapse at his side. Not possible. She had remembered something. His coat. He would freeze out here without it.

As much as she wanted to keep far away from the plane, she had no choice. The flames were visible now, licking slowly but steadily in the direction of the wings.

There was a haze of smoke in the cabin when she returned to the plane, making it difficult to see anything at all. She dared not climb inside. Stretching out her hands as far as they would reach, head averted to keep from inhaling the fumes, she felt around for his coat where he had dropped it between the front seats.

Eve had paid no attention to what their pilot had been wearing, but she remembered that Sam's coat was a dark leather. When her fingers came in contact with a smoothness that could only mean leather, she knew she had the right coat. No telling where his gun had landed when the plane crashed. Nor did she have the time to look for it.

Grabbing up the coat, she spared a last glance at the lifeless figure of Ken Redfeather. Guilt seized her at the necessity of abandoning him. It couldn't be helped.

Hugging the thick coat to her breasts, and pausing only long enough to retrieve her shoulder bag, Eve trotted back to the pine tree under which she had deposited Sam on his back. She didn't think she had the strength left in her to lift him into a sitting position and support him long enough to get him into the coat. Crouching beside him, she did the next best thing, spreading the coat over him and tucking it snugly against his sides.

The coat was enough to keep out the worst of the cold. But it was no protection when a minute later, just as she had feared, the heat of the fire reached the wings containing the fuel. There was a horrific blast, followed almost immediately by a second explosion.

Eve's reaction, when she flung herself full length over Sam's inert body, was an instinctive one. Or so she told herself. Face buried against his neck, she heard the hiss of hot metal raining down on the snow. Thankfully, none of those shards fell on them.

There was snow, too, in the air. She noticed it when she turned her head. It must have been drifting down in feathery flakes even before the crash, but Eve hadn't been conscious of it until now. It was a soft, gentle snowfall. An ironic contrast to the violence she had just experienced.

There was something else she was acutely aware of. The hardness of the body she was covering. Even through the layers of the coat, she could feel his muscular strength. More than that. With her nose pressed against the exposed skin of his throat, she was able to detect his scent. The faint, clean fragrance of his soap mingled with something masculine. Something that was distinctly Sam McDonough.

Eve had a sudden longing to do more than inhale him. A longing to flick her tongue over that warm throat where his pulse beat a seductive rhythm. A longing to taste him.

Insanity. Don't go there. Not with a man you don't like and who doesn't like you.

Hastily pulling away from him, she rolled over and sat up in the snow, drawing her knees to her chest. Tragic though it was, the fire made a welcome distraction. The crackling blaze by now had engulfed the entire plane. Several of the trees nearest the aircraft had gone up like torches, but fortunately the snow prevented the flames from spreading into the forest.

Eve knew she should be thankful for their safety. And she was. But a new reality was beginning to settle on her. A harsh one. The reality that they were on their own in the Canadian wilderness, and no one knew where they were.

Except—

A sudden recollection occurred to her. Last spring she had edited an article for her magazine about recreational aviation. The author had described the safety features of small, private airplanes. One of those features was a unit that automatically sent out signals in the event that a plane went down.

What was the thing called? Eve searched her memory. Emergency Locator Transmitter. That was it. And if Ken Redfeather's plane had been equipped with an ELT, then—

Forget it. If such a device had existed, then it would be toast by now in the conflagration that was still raging.

There could be no prospect of the plane being found and its survivors rescued. At least not by that method.

No question about it. Their plight was a dismal, desperate one. Forced down in the middle of nowhere, where the vastness was still locked in winter. An enemy somewhere out there who might not be satisfied that she was no longer a threat. And all of it complicated by a difficult man who shared this calamity with her.

Sam McDonough, who from the beginning had made no secret about what he thought of her. Never mind asking herself why. He just had.

She looked down at him, her eyes lingering on his mouth as she remembered his gruff commands to her. And even if the wide mouth that had issued those commands was the most sensual male mouth Eve had ever laid eyes on, the man behind it was still unpleasant.

This isn't helping. You can't go on sitting here like this doing nothing.

Right. But whatever decisions confronted her, they had to wait. First she needed to make some effort to rouse Sam.

And don't let yourself wonder if that might not be possible. Just do it.

How? Exactly how was she supposed to manage that? There was only one way she could think of. Getting to her knees and scooping up a handful of snow, Eve leaned over him. She started to apply the snow, but her hand paused in its descent, her gaze captured by the sight of his face.

It was a strong, compelling face beneath a thatch of dark brown hair. A seasoned face with angular features and a square jaw. There was a certain toughness about it that didn't surprise her. What she didn't expect was the complete lack of tautness. A tightness of expression that had clearly been there during his conscious state, hinting at some dark, inner struggle. Or was she just imagining the whole thing?

All right, so you're sexually attracted to this man. You'd better control your susceptibility if you don't want to get hurt.

It was a sensible instruction. Eve obeyed it as she briskly rubbed the snow over his face, hoping its wet cold would wake him. Praying he wasn't in some coma she couldn't penetrate.

"Sam," she called to him urgently, "can you hear me?"

Her treatment must have worked, but not as she'd anticipated. Instead of stirring slowly, he startled her when he came to with a sudden jerk of his body, as if shocked out of a deep sleep. The next thing Eve knew she was gazing into a pair of brown eyes with amber lights in them.

Those eyes focused on her face bent over his. There was puzzlement in them. She waited for the familiar scowl when he recognized her. She didn't get it. There was something entirely different. A grin of pleased discovery that spread across his rugged features. It was accompanied by his deep, rich voice with a low but untroubled tone that amazed her as much as the words that came out of his mouth.

"Whoever you are, angel, please tell me that we're more, *much* more, than just casual acquaintances."

Eve caught her breath in disbelief. This was a man she didn't know. She was looking into the eyes of a stranger. What on earth was happening?

When she was able to breathe again, she uttered a hoarse "You can't be serious. You must know I'm Eve. Eve Warren."

"Hello, Eve Warren," he said, caressing her name with

a slow softness that, in spite of her promise to herself, sent a warmth spreading through her whole body.

Thoroughly confused, she sat back on her heels, afraid to ask but knowing she had to. "But you remember everything else, don't you?"

"Sorry. Afraid I don't."

Her questions came swiftly then, one after the other. "Not what happened? Not where we are? But you know who you are, don't you? You have to know that."

To all of those questions, he replied by shaking his head from side to side.

His head injury from smacking so hard against the window, she thought. A trauma apparently sufficient to have short-circuited his memory. Maybe only temporarily. Maybe all she had to do was prompt him, and the rest would follow.

"You're Sam McDonough," she told him. No response. She tried again. "You're an FBI agent."

No use. He looked at her blankly. She hadn't triggered his memory. Like it or not, she had to accept his condition. God in heaven, she realized suddenly, on top of all else, she was stuck out here with a man suffering from amnesia!

He must have read the concern on her face. "Don't worry, Eve. I'm running on empty now, but I'll get it all back."

He was worried about her, not himself. What's more, his reassurance had been expressed in a kind voice. Even the smile that followed it was a pleasant one. Nothing like the hard cynicism before the crash. Was it possible that someone's attitude, perhaps his very nature as well, could change so totally like this? If so, she was ready to be thankful for it.

"The thing is—" he started to say, then broke off, his

nose wrinkling as he sniffed the air. "I smell smoke." Before she could explain, he lifted his head from the ground in order to gaze at the now-blackened remains of the plane. The flames that had consumed it were beginning to die down. "What happened?"

"We went down in the woods, and the plane caught on fire."

"Everyone get out?"

"Not our pilot. He died in the crash itself." Like Charlie, she thought, the pain of his death registering all over again. "With the plane burning as it was," she managed to explain, "there was no time for me to try to get his body out of the wreckage."

Eve didn't want to think about the loss of Ken Redfeather, the family he might have left behind. Didn't want to remind herself of Charlie and how much the memory of him hurt. She'd start to bawl if she permitted herself that lapse, and she had to hold herself together if she stood any prayer of getting out of this mess.

Sam had swung his attention away from the wreckage and was gazing at her again, this time not with concern but realization. "I was unconscious. I couldn't have helped myself out of the plane and over here on the ground. That was all you, wasn't it?"

There was gratitude in his voice. And, yes, admiration, too.

"You are some woman, Eve Warren."

His praise was unexpected. And recalling the Sam McDonough she had experienced before the crash, another complete surprise. That it had lit a glow deep inside her was probably not so good.

Eve covered her fluster with a hasty "I'm sorry I wasn't able to find and rescue your gun when I recovered your coat. But you have your passport and your wallet with your FBI ID. Maybe seeing them will help you get your memory back."

From the movement under his coat, she assumed he was feeling for the passport and wallet in his back pockets. "No, they're not in your pants pockets," she corrected him, remembering he had shoved them into a side pocket of his coat after showing them to the Mountie. "They're in one of your coat pockets."

Hands emerging from beneath the coat, he burrowed into its pockets. "No passport or wallet," he said. "Just earmuffs, a pair of gloves and a scarf."

"But they have to be there. Are you sure that— Oh, no!"

"What?"

"I was in such a rush I must have grabbed the wrong coat, thinking the pilot's coat had to be very different from yours, when all along— Oh, Sam, how could I have been so stupid?"

"You weren't stupid. Anyone could have confused them in a situation like that."

"But your passport and wallet—"

"Destroyed in the fire. So, Eve, I guess I'll just have to trust that I'm who and what you say I am. But while I'm doing that..." Coat sliding down to his waist, he lifted himself into a sitting position. It was apparently an unwise action. It was followed by a sharp "Whoa" and his hand going to the lump on the side of his head.

Eve was instantly alarmed. "How badly does it hurt?"

Sam felt around the swelling. "Has to be a souvenir from the crash."

"Your head connected with the window hard enough to crack a fairly thick pane of glass."

"Which explains my memory loss, I guess. Actually, it's just a little tender. But I do have one hell of an old-fashioned headache." He eyed her purse on the ground. "I don't suppose you'd have a couple of aspirin in there?"

"I do, but I'm not sure you should take them. You could have a concussion, and taking anything like that might not be safe."

"I'm willing to risk it. I'll have those aspirin, please."

Eve hesitated and then reluctantly reached for her bag, finding the aspirin inside and handing two of them to him. She watched him swallow the pills, washing them down with a handful of snow he scooped up from the ground. She was putting the aspirin container back in her bag when she spotted her cell phone in one corner. She had forgotten it until now.

"Look!" she said brightly, holding up the phone. "We're saved!"

But they weren't saved. When she flipped open the instrument and powered it up, the display indicated a strong battery but no signal whatsoever. What had led her to believe there possibly could be one when Ken Redfeather had complained of the scarcity of communication towers in the region?

She closed the phone and put it back in her bag. "No signal," she reported. "And no distress call from the plane, either. The pilot never got the chance to send one."

"Looks like you and I are on our own out here, Eve. Just where are we, anyway?"

"Canada. Somewhere along the British Columbia and Alberta border, so the pilot said. We were headed for Calgary, and from there…"

Eve was prepared to fill him in on all the rest. She figured he'd want to know everything from the time he met her at the ski lodge, but he halted her.

"Just what I'm doing here and why can wait. In case

you haven't noticed, the light is growing weaker, which means it must be late afternoon."

"And?"

"We have to find shelter of some kind before night closes in. It's winter, isn't it?"

"Getting on toward late April, actually. It's cold but not as cold as it was up in the Yukon where we boarded the plane. I suppose because we're much farther south now."

"Yeah, but the temperatures are bound to drop after dark. We could freeze out here."

"What are you doing?" she challenged him as he climbed to his feet and bundled into the coat.

"Trying this on for size. Not bad. A little short and a little too roomy, but it's plenty warm."

"You shouldn't be up yet."

"You think it's a lot healthier for me to have a wet backside on the ground?"

"But if you do have a concussion—"

"Maybe, but I don't think I have any of the classic symptoms."

"You have a headache."

"So would you if you smacked your head into a hard surface. It's not conclusive evidence of a concussion." He looked down at her where she was still crouched in the snow, a glint of humor in his eyes. "I love you fussing over me, angel, but don't."

Angel. He had called her *angel* again. Now why on earth, in a situation as bad as this one, should she suddenly and out of nowhere recall the memory of her mother teaching her when she was a little girl how to bake an angel food cake from scratch? How, through the years of growing up that followed, her mother had taught her so many other culinary skills. A joy that stayed with her to this day. Warm, pleasant memories. Maybe that's why she recalled them. Because at this moment she needed something that was ordinary and nonthreatening.

Sam was still gazing at her. "Have it your way," she mumbled. "Just be careful."

"I'll keep that in mind. Come on."

Before she could prevent it, he leaned down from that six-foot-plus height of his, caught her by the hand and raised her to her feet. Eve didn't need his help. She wasn't used to men helping her. She had always been independent and self-reliant. Well, maybe not with the same certainty since Charlie's cruel death. Everything had changed after that.

She waited for him to release her hand once she was standing. He didn't. He pulled her against his hard length. She felt suddenly light-headed as he pinned her there to his chest, his eyes searching hers. Not only light-headed but powerless to resist his sexual charisma. And she needed to do just that.

Thankfully, it was all over in a brief moment, although Eve was shaken when he let her go and she was able to step safely away from him.

He zipped up the coat that was now his as if nothing had happened, added the scarf, drew on the gloves from one pocket and covered his head with the earmuffs from the other pocket. His suggestion that "You might want to raise the hood on that parka" was a casual one.

How could he be so confident and unconcerned when he'd lost his memory, when calamity had landed them here where their very survival was in jeopardy? Could being relieved of your conscious memory also relieve you of your cares? Was this an explanation for the drastic change in Sam's disposition? It was a theory, anyway.

"You ready?" he asked. Eve had produced her own

gloves from her coat pocket, wriggled into them and raised her hood. "Then let's move. There's nothing more here for us."

Without waiting for her, he strode ahead through the trees. Snatching up her shoulder bag, Eve hurried after him. All right, she would admit it, at least to herself. Sam McDonough was a remarkable man. He could also be an exasperating one.

He might have lost his memory, but not the qualities that must have made him an exceptional FBI agent. Like leadership. Or had that simply been built into his character from birth? Either way, he took charge, and as long as he didn't bark orders at her, Eve let him.

One thing was evident. Sam was in no way handicapped by either his injury or the amnesia it had produced. Except to check on her at regular intervals to make sure she was okay, he never faltered in his straight, southerly course through the forest, as if certain of their destination. Was it pure instinct, Eve wondered, or did the FBI train its agents in wilderness survival?

It had stopped snowing shortly after they left the site of the wreckage, which was an advantage as far as seeing through the failing light was concerned. But the fresh powder on top of the accumulation below was not so easy to navigate. At least it wasn't for Eve, who welcomed the places under the thicker canopies of the evergreens where the white cover was thin.

The only sound was the crunch of their booted feet as they trudged through the snow. They talked infrequently and only in brief intervals, saving their wind for the trek. Even so, Eve was beginning to tire.

She was also starting to wonder if this whole thing was madness. Whatever Sam's easy assurance, maybe they were hunting for something that wasn't there. Maybe they should have stayed with the plane. Didn't pilots file flight plans? Yes, of course, they did. And when their plane didn't arrive at its destination, wouldn't a rescue team come searching for it?

But we won't be there when they find it.

Eve was about to tell Sam this. She didn't, because she understood something else then. It could be hours before anyone realized the plane was long overdue and an air search was mounted. And days after that before they located the wreckage, if ever. Long before that, she and Sam would have died of exposure. He was right. They had to find shelter of some kind, even if it was a cave.

As miserable as tramping through this endless forest was, there was one thing Eve did enjoy. The sight of Sam in front of her with his steady, long-legged gait and erectness of body, almost military in its bearing. Not to mention his tight, sexy backside, what she could see of it, anyway, in that coat.

She tried to tell herself it didn't hurt to look, though she knew her interest was a mistake. Another attraction she should be resisting. But she couldn't seem to help herself.

Even that sight, however, was no longer entertaining when her legs started to ache and her weariness had her stumbling over half-buried logs and rocks. Fearing that darkness would overtake them out here, Eve was about to break their silence and ask him just how much farther he expected them to travel when he halted abruptly.

"Look," he said, moving aside so she could see his discovery.

Light just through the trees! The last of daylight that seemed bright after the gloom of the forest. It had to be a clearing, maybe not natural, maybe man-made. And that could mean some form of civilization.

It did disclose itself as a form of civilization when they reached it a moment later. But it was no longer occupied and hadn't been in years, probably even decades.

Eve could see in the fading light that the once-sizable clearing was being reclaimed by the forest. Young pine trees were everywhere in the tall, dry weeds that long ago had likely been a field and a garden. Subsistence farming, she thought, and it had failed. Not surprising out here in the middle of nowhere.

"I think I can make out a kind of track over there leading out of the clearing," Sam said. "If so, we're in business. It must lead to a settlement somewhere. But tonight…"

"We need a shelter."

Not that she could see anything resembling one. There were the remains of a small log cabin and an adjacent outbuilding at one side of the clearing, but they offered no shelter. Their roofs had collapsed long ago, and their walls threatened to soon follow, leaving both structures wide open to the elements.

"Has to be something we can use," Sam said. "Let's look for it."

The light was fast leaving them as they crossed the clearing, but Sam seemed to have the eyes of an owl. He found that *something* near the cabin.

"What is it?" Eve wondered, peering through the twilight at a snow-covered mound.

"I'm betting it's a root cellar."

He was right. There were crude stone steps leading down to a plank door that was still intact.

"Better let me go first," he said, his booted foot scrubbing aside the snow piled on the steps as he descended to the door. "Could be some unfriendly animal has taken up residence down there."

Not an impossibility, Eve thought, since the door at the bottom of the steps was ajar by a few inches. The door was sagging, which meant Sam had to put his shoulder to it to scrape it open. Eve waited nervously at the top of the steps as, head lowered for what was presumably a low ceiling, he disappeared into the cellar. Seconds later she heard his muffled curse.

"What is it? What's wrong?"

"Nothing. I just knocked my head against something hanging from a hook in the ceiling."

Great. As if he needed another lump on his head.

"Hey, I think it's a lantern. And it still has oil in it. There's a tin of safety matches, too, on a ledge just below it."

It had to be black down there. How could he possibly make out anything?

"Let's see if they still work."

They did. A moment later the lantern bloomed with light that glowed through the open door.

"Come on down," he urged.

Eve joined him in the root cellar. The light of the lantern that Sam had placed on an overturned crate revealed a small room with a hard-packed earthen floor, the low ceiling she had anticipated and stone walls against which were ranged wooden shelves.

Sam was pleased with his find. "It's okay, huh? Below-ground like this, and with that mound over it, the temperature down here must never dip below freezing. The lantern puts out some warmth, too."

"Home never looked better," Eve agreed.

Sam found an abandoned can in one corner. He took it outside to fill with snow, which he intended to melt over the heat of the oil lantern. By the time he returned, Eve had placed two of the wide, loose shelves on the floor to serve as seats for them.

"Cozy, right?" Sam asked a short while later as they sat side by side on the boards, legs outstretched.

Eve couldn't deny, with the door now tightly shut and keeping out the worst of the cold, that the cellar made a snug refuge for them. The snow had melted in the can. He passed it to her. She drank from it and handed the can back to him. It tasted flat, but it was water. She was grateful for that.

"Too bad," Sam said after satisfying his own thirst, "they didn't leave any food behind on those shelves. Not that it would be any good by now."

"You hungry? I am, too, so..." Opening her shoulder bag, Eve produced two granola bars from its depth. "Like the Girl Scouts, I believe in coming prepared. Or is it the Boy Scouts? Doesn't matter."

She extended one of the bars toward him. Sam grabbed it with a heartfelt "Angel, you are an angel." He started to tear off the wrapper and then stopped. "This is no good."

"Why? What are you thinking?"

"If we eat both of these bars tonight, it leaves us nothing for tomorrow. Unless you have some more goodies down there."

"I don't." He was right. They needed to save something for tomorrow. Maybe even beyond tomorrow, much as she hated to think of that possibility.

"Here," he said, giving his bar back to her. "Take temptation away from me before I weaken."

With his strong will, she doubted he would. But she accepted the bar, tucking it back in her purse before she unwrapped the other bar, divided it and handed him his half.

They were silent for a moment, munching on their spare rations. Sam had asked her not to fuss about his health. She had obeyed that request while they were on the move, but now that they were safe and settled she felt a need to question him.

"Your headache—"

"Is no longer a problem. The aspirin took care of that. And please don't make an issue of the lump I'm wearing up here, either. It's still a bit sore from that hard whack against the window, but it isn't giving me any real trouble, I promise."

"Good." She hesitated before asking a cautious "Your memory, Sam. Is anything coming back?"

He thought about it for a few seconds before answering her. "There have been a few images, just these quick flashes that come and go before I can hang on to them, never mind make any sense of them. Maybe it's time we got working on that."

"You're ready to have me tell you what you're doing here and why I'm with you?"

"Might help if I can start connecting some dots."

He listened patiently, without question or comment, as Eve started from the beginning. She made her story as brief, but complete, as possible, telling him how she and Charlie Fowler were on holiday together at the Yukon skiing village. That they had traveled separately up to the village where he had left her at the end of the week to fly back home. And died on the road to the airport in Dawson, a death that the Mounties were unable to determine was accident or murder and which still had her in its emotional grip. But this last bit she kept to herself.

She did explain, however, that the Mounties had agreed on behalf of the FBI to keep an eye on Charlie Fowler. And since he'd apparently had some connection with organized crime back in the States, the RCMP had promptly contacted the bureau following his death. The bureau had sent Special Agent Sam McDonough to escort her to Chicago. Their bush plane had been shot down en route, allegedly at the orders of crime boss Victor De-Marco.

"That's everything, Sam." It wasn't. There was something more, but Eve had no intention of sharing it with the FBI. They didn't need to know it. "I'm sorry I can't tell you anything about your life before you met me at the lodge. But maybe what I have told you is sparking your memory."

Sam shook his head. "It isn't. We'll have to give it time." He was quiet for a moment. "This DeMarco character. Why is he trying to kill you?"

"I don't know," she answered truthfully.

"Okay." Having accepted that, he was thoughtful for another minute. "So, whatever the reason, we were going home to Chicago where I was to deliver you to my squad supervisor."

"Well, home for you, I suppose, but not for me. I live in St. Louis."

"And what do you do in St. Louis, Eve Warren?"

"I'm the senior editor for a regional magazine."

"Huh, impressive."

"It's not like one of the big New York magazines, Sam. We just cover the St. Louis metropolitan area—openings and restaurants and what's trendy on the local scene. Things like that."

"Family?"

"Not anymore. I just had my mother, and I lost her two years ago. My dad died when I was a teenager."

Sam murmured his sympathy. Before she could thank him for that, she felt a yawn coming on. She smothered it, wondering what time it was. She checked her watch. Well after nine o'clock already, even though some light had remained in the sky not much more than an hour ago. But then she'd forgotten how long the days were at this time of year.

"I'm exhausted."

"We could both use a solid night's sleep," he said.

She was about to agree and didn't. She had remembered something. "You can't go to sleep, not if you do have a concussion. At least not for more than an hour or two at a time. I think that's what I've heard."

She was afraid he would oppose her argument and was relieved when he agreed.

"All right, I'll take the first watch. When I can no longer keep my eyes open, I'll wake you for your shift." He leaned forward, lowering the wick on the lantern until its glow was reduced to a faint gleam. "Still plenty of oil, but it might be smart to conserve it."

Huddled together, with their backs against the wall, Eve was prepared for that solid sleep Sam had prescribed. She didn't get it. The cellar might be above freezing, but it was anything but warm. Even with the door tightly closed, she could feel currents of cold air seeping through the cracks between its planks. And although she was so tired she couldn't help dozing off, it was a fitful sleep. She kept waking up, shivering against the icy drafts that stirred around the floor.

He didn't object when, in desperation, Eve scooted against the man at her side, seeking his warmth. Sam McDonough, offering security and comfort with his presence. She valued these along with a surprising gentleness and a sense of humor, both of which had miraculously surfaced from under a brittle crust.

Eve didn't want him not to find his memory. To wish

otherwise would be unthinkable. Still, she sighed, she would regret trading this caring man for the hateful one he'd been before his amnesia, when he'd been nothing but impatient with her.

She could imagine by the way he had treated her then what he must have thought of her. Probably some kind of mercenary wanton willing to go off with an older man for what she could get out of it. If so, his judgment couldn't have been further from the truth. Eve was certainly no nun, but she did like to think she was a principled woman with decent values and she was in no way promiscuous.

This was no good. Even pressed against him like this, she was still cold, unable to drift off.

She must have made him aware of her discomfort, alerted him with her restlessness. He startled her with a softly growled "The hell with this." Zipping his coat down, he held both sides of it open to her. "Come on inside here with me."

Eve didn't hesitate to accept his invitation, unwise though her action might be. Heaven, she thought when he'd folded the sides of the coat around her and she was sprawled practically on top of him, snuggled against the welcome heat of his body.

It was more than that, though. His effect on her—all right, admit it—was downright sexy. With her face buried against his hard chest, she could hear the beat of his heart, smell his masculine aroma. It was almost more than she could bear.

He must have found it equally arousing. "If you go on squirming against me like this, something is going to happen here that one of us might not want to happen."

Oh, lord, he was right! She could feel it now, even through all the layers of their clothes. The rigid shaft of a male erection. "Sorry," she muttered.

Eve fought the temptation of him and immediately stopped wriggling. After another moment, lulled by the reassuring sound of his breathing, she managed to fall into a deep sleep.

Sam had no trouble keeping that first watch. With Eve in his arms like this, it was impossible to relax long enough to so much as drowse. Not when he was so intensely conscious of his desire for her. How soft and warm she felt nestled against him, the seductive scent of her russet hair just beneath his nose and those sweet, feminine curves. Damn, when she'd strained against him like that, he'd wanted nothing more than to bury himself deep inside her. He had almost lost it then.

Face it, McDonough. You've got the genuine hots for the lady.

Not smart. Not smart at all with this predicament they were in that had him instinctively needing to protect her. Wanting to protect her. It wasn't just duty, either. It was something much stronger than that, something beyond lust which included his irrational jealousy of a dead man he found himself battling.

Charlie Fowler. Had he been her boyfriend? It was only reasonable to suppose he must have been since they were alone together in that skiing village. And if Fowler hadn't been her lover, maybe there was someone special waiting for her back home. Hard to imagine there wouldn't be with a woman as alluring as Eve Warren.

This was nuts. He had no right to feel frustrated like this over a woman he'd known for only a few hours. Wasn't he frustrated enough by his memory loss? For all he knew, he could have someone special himself waiting back in Chicago, maybe even a wife and kids. No, he was pretty sure he didn't. He couldn't say why he was so certain, only that he sensed on some deep level he was unattached.

But, yeah, that's what he ought to be concentrating on—getting his memory back. So far all he had were those meaningless scraps. A disturbing image of a collection of paintings bathed in a low, eerie light. Then a room somewhere he didn't recognize. That was all so far.

Never mind. He'd eventually sort them out. If, that is, he managed to get Eve and him through what tomorrow might bring. With nothing but a single granola bar between them, and maybe an enemy still out there somewhere, he was going to have one hell of a job keeping them alive and Eve safe in this frozen, no-man's-land.

Chapter 3

Eve was aware of a faint but steady light in the root cellar. Not the oil lantern. The last time she'd swiveled her gaze in its direction, she had realized it must have exhausted its oil in the night. It was no longer burning.

Now, seeking the source of the light, she discovered little beams of it stealing through the narrow cracks between the planks of the door. Daylight.

The glow was just sufficient for her to read her watch. It was time for her to wake Sam again. They had traded off vigils of wakefulness during the night, with Sam registering no symptoms of a concussion. It seemed he was in the clear.

They had managed between them to get enough rest during the night. But now they needed to be on the move again. Not, however, before Eve answered another need. She had to relieve herself.

Much as she hated to leave the warmth and comfort of Sam's side, she had no other choice. It was either that or risk an embarrassing accident. She managed to remove herself from his embrace without disturbing him. It wouldn't hurt to let him go on sleeping until she returned from her errand.

Tucking the sides of his open coat over his chest, Eve got to her feet. Her intervals of slumber had permitted her to recover her strength, but her body paid the penalty of a night on the hard floor in an awkward position. She was as stiff as an old woman.

Taking a moment to restore her circulation and ease her sore muscles, she gazed down at Sam. Even like this, snoring softly and sprawled against the stone wall, he was a powerful figure. The sight of his face, shadowed with the beginning of a beard, rugged features relaxed in sleep, tugged at her with a gut-level sensation of tenderness.

You've got to stop this. It's only going to mean heartbreak for you in the end.

He didn't stir when she resolutely turned away from him, scraped the door back and climbed out of the cellar. The morning sunlight glinting off the snow was so brilliant it was blinding. No wonder. When she shaded her eyes against the glare with her hand, she saw that the sky had cleared in the night and was now a sharp, pure blue.

What last evening's twilight and overcast sky had failed to reveal was plainly visible this morning. Far away, above the forest, rose a majestic mountain range. Beautiful, but at this moment there was something more important within easy reach. Behind the remains of the log cabin, and overlooked by them last night, was a weathered privy.

With a silent thanks to whoever had built the tiny

structure, Eve hastened across the clearing. Like the root cellar, the privy was still miraculously intact.

After using the facility, and in the absence of water, she had no choice but to wash her hands with the clean snow. Frigid though it was, she scrubbed her face with snow, too.

Refreshed, she started back across the clearing in the still, frosty air. Sam had emerged from the root cellar and was standing at the top of the steps. He grinned at her when she reached him.

"I missed you," he greeted her. "Where were you?"

"Had to answer the call of nature. In case you, ah, also…" She finished her explanation by nodding in the direction of the privy.

Sam lost no time in following her example. When he returned, he no longer wore the grin. It had been replaced by a slight frown.

"You should have roused me, Eve. We should have been on the move long ago."

He must have consulted his own watch. She answered him with a pointedly sweet "Good morning to you, too."

The grin returned, this time a sheepish one. "Sorry," he mumbled.

There would have been no grin, no apology from the other Sam McDonough, she thought. Just a scowl. No, she didn't want him not to recover his memory, but she knew that when he did, she would no longer feel this warmth in his company.

"No breakfast before we leave?" she asked, thinking of the second granola bar in her purse.

"We'd better save it for later on."

Meaning when their need could no longer be ignored. Eve realized he was right.

After sharing the last of the melted water in the can,

they set off across the clearing. The track that Sam had been confident last night existed proved to be a reality in the light of day.

The forest immediately swallowed them as they followed the rough lane that wound away toward the south. Narrow though the track was, it permitted them to walk side by side. But they spoke only occasionally and, as if by silent agreement, never about last night's intimacy in the root cellar.

Just as well, Eve decided. It had no meaning this morning. Or so she made every effort to tell herself. After all, this Sam was not the real one. Sooner or later, he would regain his memory. The true Sam would emerge again, the one she wanted no part of, whatever her physical attraction to him.

Suddenly, Eve heard it. The throb of beating blades somewhere above the forest. She halted, dragging at Sam's arm with a tense "Hear it?"

He nodded soberly. "I hear it."

"It's a helicopter, isn't it?"

"Sounds like it."

"It could be a rescue helicopter hunting for us."

"Or that enemy chopper you told me about."

Eve had already feared that possibility, too. "What should we do?"

"Nothing. Even if it is a friendly craft, there's no way we can signal it from down here under all these trees. And no way they can spot us either in all this heavy growth."

Nor did Eve have any desire for such a contact. Not if that helicopter *was* connected with Victor DeMarco.

The sound faded to a hum in the distance, and finally the sky was silent once more. Eve kept listening for it as she and Sam went on, but it never approached them again. The hours passed, the sun moving over to the west. And all the while, as they tramped onward through the snow, the granola bar in Eve's purse spoke to her.

When she could no longer ignore its call, or the ache in her legs, she demanded a break. "I'm hungry, and I'm tired."

"You're right. It's time for a rest stop."

They found a thick log around a bend in the trail. Sam brushed the snow off the top of it, and they perched on it side by side. Eve divided the bar and gave him his half of it.

She ate her share with relish, refusing to let herself remember this was the last of their food. Or, for that matter, to worry about slowly starving out here in all this frozen vastness.

Eve resolutely turned to Sam and broached another subject. "Any luck yet regaining your memory?"

The Adam's apple in his throat bobbed as he swallowed the last of his ration. She found something erotic about that sight. No man had ever had this kind of effect on her before. It was exciting, but foolish. Wasn't it? Yes, of course, it was.

He shook his head. "Just those pieces that still have no meaning for me. When I do have something worthwhile, I'll let you know."

She understood him. He was telling her he would prefer she stop questioning him about it. Probably the state of the lump on the side of his head, as well. No need anyway to ask about that. She could see that the swelling had lessened considerably.

"You ready to go on?"

She hesitated.

"What?"

"Sam, what if this excuse for a road doesn't lead us anywhere? Anywhere useful, that is."

"Has to. Whoever built that cabin and farmed the clearing would have needed a way in and out to someplace where they could buy the supplies they couldn't grow. Only makes sense." He gazed at her when she didn't answer him. "You're still skeptical about it, aren't you?"

"I didn't say that."

"You didn't have to. Your eyebrows told me."

"My what?"

"Eyebrows." He smiled at her, the amber lights in his brown eyes glinting with humor. "No matter how controlled the expression on your face might be, your eyebrows give you away. Hasn't anyone ever told you that?"

"No. Just what are my eyebrows saying now?"

"One of them is lowered, the other is raised. You aren't sure what to believe. Adds up to uncertainty. See?"

She had to give him points for being exceptionally observant. FBI training maybe. From now on, she'd have to try not to let her eyebrows betray her. There were some feelings she'd rather he didn't know about.

"So, we go on?" he said.

She'd much rather stay right here and lean her head on his broad shoulder.

Not a good desire, Eve. And watch those eyebrows.

She got to her feet. "We go on."

The afternoon lengthened as they trekked onward. She was tired from this ceaseless tramping, but she refused to complain about it. She tried not to think what would happen when the sun went down. But it was impossible to keep from wondering if they would have to spend their second night out in the open. They might not be lucky enough this time to find another clearing offering a snug refuge.

To her amazement, they did reach another clearing. It was considerably larger than the one that was now miles behind them. And much brighter. Light enough to show them it was not man-made this time, but a natural meadow in the forest. Nowhere in its expanse was there any indication of a possible shelter.

They had no choice but to cross the clearing to the track that meandered on through the endless forest. Sam's hand held her back at the edge of the woods when they reached that track.

"Let me have your cell phone."

"Why? It doesn't display any signal."

"You haven't tried it again. We've traveled far enough that maybe this time it will."

Eve dug the cell phone out of her bag and handed it to him.

"Wait here for me."

"Gladly." She was more than ready for another rest stop. A large boulder a few feet away beckoned to her. Sweeping away the snow, she sank gratefully onto its flat surface.

Sam took the phone and moved back out into the clearing. She watched his tall figure from her perch as he halted yards away from her, opened the phone, powered it up and squinted at the display. There couldn't have been any signal. That's why he held it higher and began to turn around slowly, seeking some kind of signal.

Eve saw the sun, low in the sky now, strike golden sparks off the metal of the upraised phone. It made a peaceful sight. Or did, until mere seconds later the stillness was shattered by the crack of a rifle. To her dismay, the cell phone seemed to come apart in Sam's raised hand.

Dropping the now-useless instrument, he shouted to her, "Take cover!" Without pause, he sprinted back toward her at top speed, dodging a hail of bullets as he ran. A perfect target, she thought, heart in her throat as she sprang to her feet. "Cover!" he yelled again.

Eve didn't hesitate this time. She dived behind the boulder, squeezing her knees up to her chest to make herself as small as possible. Her brain was rapidly at work again.

She had seen no sign of the shooter. Or maybe there was more than one of them. Whoever they were, and she was already almost 100 percent certain of their identity, they must have crept up on them and were hidden now in the trees on the far side of the clearing.

To her relief, Sam joined her behind the boulder, dropping flat at her side.

"Were you hit? Please tell me you weren't hit."

"I wasn't hit. But we will be if we don't get out of here."

Bidding her to follow him, he led the way, crawling rapidly on his belly into the trees behind them.

"You know who they are, don't you?" she called to him breathlessly.

"Oh, yeah. The boys from that chopper."

"They must have finally sighted the wreckage of the plane."

"More likely the clearing where we spent the night. And if they came in low for a closer look, our tracks in the snow would have been plainly visible. All they had to do was set down there and follow our trail."

"They'll come after us, of course."

"You can bet on it." Reaching the edge of the lane, Sam climbed to his feet. Eve joined him. "No more talk now. We need to save our breath if we're going to stand any chance of losing them."

She fearfully wondered if that was possible when their bootprints would leave another clear trail. And, worse than that, the enemy had the firepower to bring them down.

Grabbing her hand, Sam ran with her swiftly along the trail. With her mounting fatigue, Eve silently questioned how long she could keep up with him. Just how far behind them were their pursuers? Even moving cautiously, it wouldn't take them long to cross the clearing and find the trail on the other side.

She and Sam couldn't have gone more than a few hundred yards along the curving trail when he abruptly stopped. She drew up beside him, glad for the opportunity to catch her breath.

"This is no good," he muttered. "With these tracks we're leaving, we're practically inviting them to catch up to us."

He looked quickly to the left, then the right. They had entered a region where the forest was dominated by tall pines on both sides of the trail. The trees grew so close together that the snow barely penetrated the dense, evergreen boughs high above, and then only laying down scattered patches of crusty white in the forest itself. Most of its floor was thickly carpeted with nothing but dry needles.

Eve understood Sam's intention. They would leave no tracks in the pine forest. She also understood what he was doing when he began to scuff up the snow from the middle to the edge of the trail on their left where the clean needles began.

She needed no urging to help him. She took the right side. Within seconds, they had created a confusion of bootprints clear across the trail, making it impossible for their pursuers to figure out on which side she and Sam had entered the forest.

"The left side, I think," he directed her. "Stomp your boots before we go in. We don't want to shed any traces of snow in there."

With the towering pines shutting out what sunlight remained, *in there* proved to be as dim and shadowy as dusk. It was also as silent as a church, which was probably why Eve whispered her nervous "Where are they? I don't hear anything."

"Wasting time arguing over which direction we took, I hope."

They plunged onward into the depths of the forest, careful to avoid the rare patches of snow. Eve was determined not to give voice to her weariness as they zigzagged though the endless ranks of the pines. But her strength had already been sapped by a long day of hiking, and the last of it was ebbing fast.

Although she said nothing, her increasingly sluggish steps were a clear indication of her exhaustion. Sam halted them. "You're ready to collapse."

"It's all right. I can go on."

"No, you can't."

"Maybe if we just rest for a bit."

"Can't afford to chance it. They could already have picked up our trail, and if they catch up to us…" She could see he was thinking of a solution. Seconds later, looking first left, then right, he was apparently seized by an idea. "Over there," he said, jerking his thumb toward a shallow hollow a few yards to the right of them.

Waiting for him to explain, Eve followed him into the hollow. He hunkered down, digging his hands into the pine needles.

"The needles are much deeper here," he said. "They must have been collecting in this low spot for decades, practically filling it up." Getting down on his hands and knees, he began to swiftly claw away the layers of needles, raking them back like a dog attacking an animal's burrow. "Help me," he said.

She joined him on the other side of the depression he was creating, falling to her knees to share in the labor. "What on earth are we doing?" she asked, piling needles behind her.

"We're making a bed for you."

"We are doing *what?*"

"Eve, you're in no state to go on. I've got to cover you with needles and leave you hidden here while I lead them away."

She panicked at the prospect of his deserting her. "Sam, no! We can both hide under the needles! Anyway, maybe they won't come."

"They'll come," he said with a grim certainty. "And when they do, I want them to keep on coming."

"After *you*. They'll shoot you if they catch up to you. Sam, don't sacrifice yourself like this."

"Something tells me I like life too much for that. They won't catch me. No more arguing. This is deep enough and long enough now to fit you. Dry enough, too. In you go."

Much as she didn't like his plan, Eve was too spent to make any further objections. She felt like a corpse in a coffin once she was stretched out flat on her back in the depression. Sam began to rapidly mound the needles they had removed over her.

"I'm leaving a little gap up here so you can breathe without trouble. Whatever you hear, don't move. Not a muscle," he cautioned.

That would be a challenge, she knew. She heard him getting to his feet.

"I'll come back for you, angel. Count on it."

And then he was gone.

If anyone ever asked her what it was like to be buried alive, Eve could tell them. Not pleasant. Not pleasant at all. She understood perfectly now the experience of claustrophobia. And a sense of abandonment.

There were two advantages to her situation. She could freely breathe fresh air, and she was warm. Not so odd really, considering the sun had shone down strongly on the area all day, leaving the still air mild in temperature, even late in the day like this. Besides, the blanket of pine needles covering her made an excellent insulation.

She was comfortable enough. Physically. Emotionally, she was something else. Through the long, lonely moments, she alternated between a fear that the enemy would arrive and a hope that they would come and relieve this awful suspense she was suffering.

The minutes dragged on in a silence so absolute it was eerie. Why wasn't she hearing something? The rustle of a small animal in the brush, the snapping of a frosted branch heavy with ice. Nothing.

Maybe Sam was wrong. Maybe they wouldn't come. How could they possibly track them in all this expanse of forest when she and Sam had left no prints this time, when darkness was closing in? They couldn't.

But Sam had been right. Like wolves able to scent the direction of their prey, the enemy did come. Eve went rigid in her temporary grave when she heard the soft thud of approaching feet. And then suddenly they were there. Close, not more than a few yards away. But, mercifully, not close enough to take notice of the mound in the hollow.

There were two of them. She could tell that from their hurried exchange. Although she couldn't make out what they were saying, she was able to distinguish the quality of their voices. One had what sounded like a European accent. What country in Europe she couldn't say. The other had a deep nasal tone, as if he had a cold.

And then there was nothing. The footsteps moved off. Toward the south, she thought. The direction in which Sam had gone. She was alone again and safe. But not free of concern. She kept waiting to hear the bark of a rifle off in the distance. A chilling sound that would mean they had sighted Sam, that they possibly were able to bring him down.

But the rifle was silent. The worst of her strain gradually diminished. She grew restless, wanting to burst free of her confinement. She didn't. Much as she hated waiting, not knowing what was happening, she went on obeying Sam's direction to stay where she was.

Time passed, an eternity of it. It had to be full night by now. She brushed away enough of the needles to clear her view, expecting to see nothing but darkness. To her surprise, a silver light filtered down through the pines. The strong light of what must be a full moon.

The moonlight, together with the aroma of the pines, was soothing. She was able to relax her tense muscles. But not her mind. With nothing to do but think, her mind was busy. Random thoughts that went first in one direction, and then another. But always Sam McDonough was the subject of those emotional searches.

Only now, when she was without him, did Eve realize just how much she had come to depend on him.

What's happened to that willful independence of yours?

All right, so these were extraordinary circumstances. She had a right to depend on Sam. He was an FBI agent, wasn't he? Assigned to safeguard her until he delivered her to his squad supervisor in Chicago? And maybe, when all was said and done, they had come to count on each other.

You don't believe that, do you? It's more than that— much more.

Remembering last night in the root cellar, it was a truth she had to acknowledge. Even back at the plane wreckage she had felt it—this special attachment to Sam, this attraction for a sexy, forceful man that was more than just lust. That had her yearning for him on some deeply emotional level.

Did Sam feel it, too? She hoped he did. She had sensed he might when his arms had enveloped her in the root cellar.

There are the demons that haunt him, Eve.

Nonsense. Just because she had observed a fleeting bleakness in his eyes when they'd first met, had been conscious of a stress in his taut expression, didn't mean that beneath his current state of amnesia he suffered some secret torment. What kind of evidence was that?

A hollow one, that's what.

You know you're falling for him. You'd better watch it. It's not safe.

Yes, that was true, too. She did need to be careful. It would be so easy to involve herself both physically and emotionally with this Sam McDonough. But what would happen when the other Sam McDonough returned, the hard-edged one whose eyes didn't spark with humor? That Sam McDonough could seriously hurt her.

Oh, Sam, Sam, where are you when I need you?

How could he possibly—FBI training or not—find his way back to her at night, even with the moonlight to guide him?

Along with all this wild seesawing of worried thoughts and mixed feelings was her memory of Charlie and, whatever his connection with a crime boss, how kind and generous he had been to her. How she continued to mourn him. And probably always would.

Eve didn't know how long she waited there before she once again caught the muted sound of approaching footsteps. Had their pursuers returned, or could it be—

The footsteps suddenly stopped. She stiffened with both anticipation and apprehension.

A few seconds later, a husky whisper called out to her, "Eve, where are you?"

She had never heard a voice so welcome. Shoving herself up from the pine needles and onto her knees, she cried a glad, "Over here, Sam! I'm over here!"

With several long, eager strides he was with her, falling to his own knees in front of her. All restraint vanished in a rush of joy as her arms reached out to him. His own arms wrapped around her, gathering her against him tightly.

Their reunion was simultaneously sweet and savage as, head lowered, he covered her face with kisses. Eve had never experienced such wonderful kisses. Feverish kisses of both relief and their growing feelings for each other. Kisses of the longings of two souls seeking a connection beyond just the physical. And in between each of them they managed quick, breathless snatches of explanation.

"I heard them nearby and I was terrified they'd caught up with you. That you were dead."

"Would I do that to you? Never." He kissed a sensitive area at the side of her neck, making her shiver with delight. "I managed to outrun them."

"Where—" Eve sucked in her breath as his mouth traveled to her jaw, then her cheeks. She exhaled slowly, weakly. "Where are they now, do you suppose?"

"Gave up for the night, I imagine, and returned to their chopper. What else could they do?"

His lips had found her eyes, which she closed to accommodate him. He began to tenderly kiss each lid. Trembling, she croaked, "But they'll be back, won't they? They won't quit."

"Yeah, sooner or later they'll be back. But by then we'll be long gone. Has anyone ever told you you have the most beautiful eyes?"

"Not lately. I don't know how you ever found your way back here."

"The moonlight helped. That and a few landmarks. I may not remember my past, but I did remember those landmarks." His lips left her eyelids and moved downward along the side of her nose. "And your nose. That's beautiful, too."

"Sam, we can't—"

"No more talk now. Let me concentrate."

His mouth settled beside her own. But only for a second. Only long enough for him to slowly cross that fraction of an inch between his mouth and hers. He was deliberately torturing her. Eve was on fire with impatience until his mouth finally, fully, claimed hers.

His kiss was more than she could have imagined. A passionate action that involved his teeth nipping gently at her lower lip, then the tip of his tongue licking that same lip and finally his mouth grinding against hers, demanding her response. She obediently parted her mouth, inviting his entry.

Sam complied by sliding his tongue inside, seeking and finding her own tongue. And when he deepened their kiss with an exquisite mating of their tongues, Eve lost all self-control.

It was madness, of course. How could she forget the promise to herself not to get involved with him on this level? That it was dangerous, that when his amnesia lifted he would no longer want her. Nor was she apt to want him. An outcome that would be painful for both of them.

But it was useless. She was helpless. In spite of every warning to herself, she ignored her inner voice and surrendered to the raw pleasure of their kiss, relishing the heat of him, along with his pure, masculine flavor.

When in the end his mouth lifted from hers, Eve was so limp that she would have collapsed if his arms hadn't been supporting her. He rested his brow against hers for a long moment, rocking her slowly. A low chuckle rumbled out of him.

"You were saying?"

She was so dazed that for a few seconds she didn't know what he was talking about. Then, understanding, she dragged her head back.

"Thanks to you, Special Agent McDonough, I don't have a clue what I was talking about. Wait, yes, I do. I was starting to tell you that we can't possibly move on tonight, even with the moonlight."

"You're right. We'll spend the night here and then go on at first light."

Eve looked around her. "Right here?"

"Sure. You were warm enough, weren't you?" he said, indicating the depression in which he had buried her.

"Actually, I was."

"Then you'll be even warmer with me beside you."

The thought of him lying close beside her, sharing his body heat, was unsettling. It was also irresistible.

"Come on," he said, "help me widen and lengthen this thing."

It took them only a short time to scrape out enough pine needles to permit the excavation to accept both of them.

"We'll take off our coats," he suggested, "and use them as blankets. A double layer over the both of us should be all we need to keep from freezing."

He was right. The cavity made a snug bed with them settled in it side by side, their shed coats covering them and the excess pine needles pulled in against their sides.

Hand cupping her chin, he turned her face toward his. His mouth again descended on hers. This time, however, his kiss was not a fierce one. Nor a lengthy one. His lips against hers were feather-light but no less pleasant.

A good-night kiss, she thought. She was wrong. Although his mouth left her, his hand did not. It slid under the coats and down to her breasts where he began to caress her soft, swollen flesh. Even with the barrier of her sweater and bra, Eve felt her nipples grow instantly hard. She couldn't prevent the moan that escaped from her throat, nor her strangled plea that followed it.

"What are you doing to me?"

"Something I want you to like," he whispered.

His hand didn't stop at her breasts. It went on, dropping to her belly, which he slowly circled. Only when he reached the waistband of her slacks did his hand pause, as if he were giving her time to understand and sanction his intention.

Already in another daze, Eve didn't understand. Not,

anyway, until that skillful hand of his burrowed its way beneath her slacks, then her panties. She gasped when she felt the heat of his palm in direct contact now with her vulnerable flesh.

Before she could object, or even decide whether she wanted to object, his hand dipped lower, his fingers stirring through the nest of curls at the juncture of her thighs.

"Sam, this is—" She couldn't get the words out.

"Do you want me to stop? I'll stop if you want me to."

No, she didn't want him to stop. A mistake though this might be in every way, she didn't want him to stop. He must have read her silent assent, because his probing fingers searched onward until he found the petals of her cleft. Gently, he parted those folds, inserting his middle finger inside the center of her being. She was already wet, her nub swollen and throbbing as he began to tenderly stroke her.

Eve lost herself in a delirium of yearning, her need for release mounting, mounting. In the end, when the first spasms seized her, she bucked and arched upward, beyond all control as she rode wave after wave of indescribable pleasure.

"You're beautiful, angel," he told her. "You're beautiful in every way."

She was shaking, unable to respond until her body was at last quiet. "Sam, what about you? We haven't…satisfied you."

"Not here. Not now. We'll get to me later. We'll save the best for both of us until then. That's a promise."

He seemed so sure there would be a *later*. She wanted to believe that. *Did* believe it, even though that kind of thinking could end in grief for her.

He had called her beautiful. Eve knew she was no better looking than scores of other women. But every woman liked to feel she was special in some way, and Sam made her feel just that. Special.

On that satisfying note, secure in his embrace, warm and satiated as never before, she slept.

Like last night in the root cellar, Sam was unable to let himself fall asleep. Not for a while, anyway. His mind was too active. Eve, of course.

Hell, McDonough, can't you think of anything else?

No, he couldn't. He was responsible for her.

Yeah, like that's what's on your mind.

Okay, so it wasn't. Not at this moment. At this moment, it was plain lust. Well, that and all these tender feelings he had for her that went beyond more than just his need to protect her.

You could have had her. She was more than willing.

Sure, but he wasn't. All right, so maybe he was a fool, but it was just as he said. When he made full love to her, he wanted it to be perfect in every way. Reliably warm and comfortable, for one thing, and, for another, with no article of clothing between them. Eve deserved that. Until then, he'd just have to endure this misery of self-denial.

If she has to be in your thoughts, then try to make them a little more pure. Things like how much you've come to admire her spirit and her endurance.

It was true. He did admire those qualities in her. Thing was, he couldn't seem to separate those qualities from her looks, and that was a direction that meant trouble.

He should turn his mind to something useful. Like how he was going to get them out of this mess. It would help if he could only get his memory back.

He'd made a little more progress with that tonight while evading his pursuers. He'd pictured himself in that place again where the paintings were. This time he had realized that something very bad happened there, but he had yet to know what. He'd also recalled that other room with its view of a city street. Could now identify it as the living room of his apartment in Chicago.

But there had been nothing else. He'd have to keep working on it until he regained his full memory. Only then would he know the information his squad supervisor must have shared with him before he'd sent him off to the Yukon. Things like why Eve was so important to this Victor DeMarco character.

As it was, Sam had nothing to rely on but what Eve had told him. That she didn't know why DeMarco wanted her either dead or captured. He had no reason to believe she hadn't been telling him the truth.

If those two goons of DeMarco's had been trying to shoot their plane down, he could only surmise they'd wanted to kill Eve, as they'd allegedly killed Charlie Fowler. But Sam couldn't be sure of that.

He recalled what else Eve had told him. That their plane had dived into a cloud cover to lose the helicopter. Which meant their enemy wouldn't have known what happened to them after that. Sam could only guess they had heard afterwards that a bush plane didn't arrive in Calgary as scheduled and was presumed to be down somewhere in the wilderness with possible survivors.

One of those survivors could be Eve Warren, and that was all DeMarco's boys needed to put them hot on Eve's trail.

And that means you'd better stop worrying over what you can do nothing about tonight and get some sleep.

Oh, yeah, he would have to be rested for tomorrow. Because he was going to need all his resources if he were to have any chance of getting Eve safely away from the threat to her. And considering how much she was beginning to matter to him, that was imperative.

Chapter 4

The first gray light of daybreak was filtering through the pines when Eve awoke with a start. What was she doing out here in the open like this? For a few seconds she was too disoriented to understand, and then she remembered. She and Sam were on the run.

Her memory of the last two days' events, however, didn't explain what had so sharply awakened her. Danger? Their two armed pursuers creeping up on them?

Her body tensed when she heard a cry off through the trees. When it sounded again, she realized what it was. Nothing more than the call of a jay. Eve relaxed when the jay's mate shrilled an answer, convincing her it was the two birds that had roused her.

Turning her head, she found herself nose to nose with Sam. The jays hadn't disturbed him. His eyes were still closed. She knew she should wake him, that they needed to be on the move. But she couldn't resist stealing a moment to examine his face.

She liked what she saw under that thatch of tousled hair. The curve of the sensual mouth that had kissed her so robustly last night, robbing her of all reason. The strong, chiseled features at peace in sleep.

All so different from the hard face of the Sam McDonough before his amnesia. That Sam, even when he was still, had been like an idling engine, restless, ready to roar. But the face of this Sam, although as rugged as before his memory loss, was somehow fresh, as if he had been born all over again.

You've got to stop this before it's too late.

Where on earth was her self-restraint? But she knew the answer to that, didn't she? Sam McDonough had destroyed it.

The raucous cries of the jays hadn't awakened him, but her long sigh of appreciation must have. Those smoldering, brown eyes, with a suggestion of humor in them, were suddenly looking into hers. It was a wonderful moment of silent connection, conveying— What?

Never mind. This wasn't a time for probing minds— either his or her own. Sam must have understood that, too, when he stirred from their bed of pine needles, helping her to her feet.

"You ready to head out?" he asked her as they bundled into their coats.

She would have been, if only she had something to eat first. But there was no food. She realized he must be as hungry as she was, but he didn't complain about it. Nor would she, not when he was measuring her with a concerned look on his face. Probably wondering whether she had enough stamina for what could be another arduous trek.

"I am," she assured him brightly, "except for one thing."

"What would that be?"

"Which way do we go?"

"South again," he said without hesitation.

He seemed so certain of the direction that she felt he must have a good reason for his choice. But before she could ask him about it, he struck out ahead of her through the pines. She hurried to reach him.

She didn't try to talk to him after that, saving her wind for the pace he set to get them out of the area as quickly as possible. There was another reason for her silence. She figured that Sam was listening intently for any sound that might tell him their two friends were tracking them again. Eve was also alert for any sign of trouble, but there was no evidence of renewed pursuit. Yet.

The dense cover of pines thinned after another mile or so, becoming a mix of conifers and leafless hardwoods. They could see the sky clearly now. No sun this morning. It was overcast, threatening snowfall again. Being more in the open like this, they were vulnerable to the rifle power of the enemy. There was one advantage to this openness, though. Sufficient snow on the ground to satisfy their thirst, even if that same snow did leave a trail of their bootprints.

Eve didn't expect to welcome another snowfall, but that's just what she did when the first flakes began to drift down, obliterating their tracks behind them. Gentle though those flakes were in the beginning, they did, in time, make the going tougher.

She knew she should be concentrating on nothing but putting one foot in front of the other and not wasting her energy on anything else. But her mind couldn't seem to obey that order. She found it dwelling on all her emotions, stemming from what she and Sam had shared last night. Did it have any significance at all for the future? Or had it been just two people reaching out to each other in desperate circumstances? Something that was certain to evaporate when his memory returned?

"Thank God," she whispered under her breath when Sam finally called for a rest break.

They sheltered under a huge spruce, seating themselves side by side on a log. Eve felt she was free to speak now.

"I'm not foolish enough to celebrate, but is it possible we've lost our friends?"

"We've managed to shake them for now, but they're out there somewhere."

"Any theories on that?"

He shrugged. "Maybe just waiting for the snow to clear so they can try finding us again in the chopper. They certainly can't take to the air in this weather."

Eve had another question for him. "Is it my imagination, or has the land been sloping gradually downward? Not that I'm objecting, mind you. Down is certainly better than up."

"You're not imagining it. I noticed it last night when I managed to outrun the goons on our tail. I'm thinking we've entered a drainage area."

"Which means?"

"That there's a stream ahead of us. And if there is, it's bound to lead somewhere. Like a settlement of some kind on a riverbank."

"Ah, that's why you chose this direction."

"Hopefully, it's there and within our reach."

If we don't perish first from hunger and cold, she thought, but she didn't put that into words. She noticed he was looking at her and that he had a big, goofy grin on his face. "What?"

"Hate to tell you, angel, but your nose is running."

She would have resented any other man calling her *angel* like this all the time, but from Sam it felt good.

"Oh, great—just what a woman wants to hear. That her nose is leaking." She opened her shoulder bag and began to search through its contents. "I know I have tissues in here somewhere, but wouldn't you know I can't find one when I need it."

"Maybe Ken Redfeather carried a supply." His hands began to grope through the pockets of the coat he had inherited from their pilot. He was digging into a breast pocket when she noticed a strange look cross his face.

"Something wrong?"

"Uh, no. Sorry, there don't seem to be any tissues in the coat."

"It's all right. I've found my package of them."

It was true he hadn't located any tissues in the pilot's coat. But what he had discovered buried in the depths of that breast pocket had been far more interesting, he thought as they continued on their way. And potentially useful. He hoped.

It would have been just a bit too obvious if he'd gone and withdrawn any of those foil-wrapped packets. Not that Sam had needed to do that, anyway. His fingers were familiar enough with the product to tell him exactly what they were. Condoms.

Ol' Ken Redfeather, he decided with a private little chuckle, must have been planning a good time for himself after he delivered them to their destination. For all Sam knew, the pilot had had a girlfriend waiting for him down in Calgary. Too bad that connection would never happen now.

Sad really, and not something he should be chuckling about. Especially when he had so much else to occupy his attention. The weather, in particular. Not only was it snowing harder with a rising wind, but the temperature had plummeted to a frigid level. He was worried about Eve.

"How are you doing?" he asked her.

"Managing. But a pair of skis would make the going a lot easier. The downhill variety."

She was right. They were currently descending a long hill, where the snow was building so rapidly that plowing through it was increasingly difficult.

The hill sparked another memory for him, this time from his boyhood. He could see himself sledding down just such a hill and out across a frozen pond. Somewhere in rural Michigan, he thought. He must have been raised in Michigan.

He hoped for other breakthroughs to follow that one, but none occurred. He'd just have to be patient and wait for them.

"Is it only in the desert that you see a mirage?" she wondered, peering ahead of them through the falling curtain of white. "Or is it possible to see one in a snowstorm?"

"I wouldn't know. Why?"

"Because it's either a mirage I'm seeing down there, or it's that stream you promised me."

Sam could see it now, too, below them. The stream that proved his faith in the existence of one. It wasn't a mirage either, but a reality. From what he could tell in the driving snow when they reached its bank, it was a narrow, winding river, its solidly frozen waters offering them an open highway through the wilderness.

"Which way?" Eve asked him.

"To the left. And don't ask me why. It just feels to me like that's downstream, and downstream seems better than upstream."

"Well, you've been right so far, so let's do it."

She sounded enthusiastic enough about his decision, but Sam's concern about her deepened with the snow as they followed the river. He could see she was growing tired. He needed to find a refuge for them, one that provided food. But there was no sign of any habitation, nothing but the endless, unbroken forest on either side.

In one way the river was in their favor. Except for occasional drifts, around which they were either able to detour or had no choice but to wallow through, the wind had swept the ice clean of such obstacles. But that same wind punished them with a biting cold.

Hell, why not call it what it was? A genuine, freaking blizzard. At least there was no helicopter diving down on them. Not in this stuff. But there was Eve and his fears for her. She was struggling along bravely at his side. But her progress was an uncertain one, requiring his steadying hand whenever she stumbled, which was happening more frequently as they advanced.

There was something else Sam didn't like. Instead of saving her breath, she began to talk. And of all things, considering they had eaten nothing since yesterday, what she talked about was food.

"Do you like bread pudding, Sam?" She gave him no chance to respond. "The secret ingredient for my bread pudding is molasses. It's no secret down in Louisiana. Molasses bread pudding is a very popular dessert in Louisiana."

"Is that so?"

"Oh, yes. I know a lot about Louisiana cooking. I hope one day to operate my own restaurant featuring Louisiana dishes. Not the trendy Creole and Cajun fare, but genuine down-home cooking. I think the Midwest could use a restaurant like that, don't you?"

"What happened to being a senior editor of a magazine?"

"That was never my dream. I just kind of drifted into it. See, I was freelancing reviews of metro-area restaurants, and the magazine liked my writing. They needed an assistant editor and offered me the job. The money was good, and what with Mom's Parkinson's disease getting worse, that was important. Then when the senior editor left the magazine, and the salary for that position was even more tempting…"

"The dream got lost."

"Not lost, Sam. *Put on hold.* I'll get back to it one day. I'm a very good chef. Chicken gumbo and rice is one of my specialties. Rice is a staple in Louisiana. They grow it there, you know."

He found it interesting that she was sharing all these revelations about herself, even though this was hardly the occasion for them. With his memory still largely untapped, he was able to offer nothing worthwhile about himself in response. All he could do was listen and worry.

Eve was huffing with exertion by now. He should have tried to silence her, but she seemed to need to talk. He humored her, letting her ramble on cheerfully about sweet potato pone.

But that was a mistake. He realized that when, describing something called shrimp remoulade for him, her phrases began to get repeatedly disjointed.

"Shrimp...that's a Louisiana staple, too...bet you know that already, Sam...everybody knows that...I think they do...but not about the hard-boiled eggs maybe...no, not about the hard-boiled eggs...minced very fine, those eggs should be..."

Yeah, it was a mistake. She was beginning to sound almost delirious. Dazed by hunger and exhaustion. He had to get her out of this miserable weather. But how, where?

From what he could tell in the blinding snow, there was still nothing out there but the forest. No shape of anything resembling a shelter for them.

He'd lost all awareness of how far they had traveled on the frozen stream. It might have been a considerable distance or only a couple of miles. All he knew for certain was that their situation had become dire.

The conditions couldn't be any worse than what they already were, he thought. Or maybe they could, he realized when they rounded a bend in the stream and found themselves suddenly confronted by a barrier.

"A wall, Sam! Isn't that strange? What's a wall doing here in the river?"

It wasn't a wall, not in the sense that Eve meant. No human hands were responsible for it. It had been constructed by nature out of earth, rock and uprooted trees. A high, solid arm flung across the width of the stream, leaving only a narrow gap on the far right side through which the waters must have flowed before they froze. That gap now was choked by a pile of tumbled chunks of ice, some of them as large as boulders.

Yeah, Sam was able to understand what had happened, but only because the snowfall thinned for a few moments, permitting him to see the enormous wound against the hillside, which rose so steeply and sharply off the left bank of the river that no snow had collected there. A wound still so raw that the upheaval must have occurred as recently as last fall before the land had frozen, leaving the area stripped of all growth.

"It isn't a wall, Eve," he corrected her. "It's the result of a landslide, and we have no choice but to climb over it. Think you can manage?"

"Will there be anything on the other side worth climbing over for, Sam?"

"I hope so, angel. I hope so."

What else could he tell her, even if he expected them to find nothing on the other side but what they already had on this side? More of the same. But that wasn't the point. The point was to keep going. He couldn't permit them to do otherwise. Not as long as there was any chance of survival.

"Then I'll try," she promised him.

But her flagging strength matched neither her courage nor her willingness to continue. Even with his assistance, his gloved hand drawing her up over the tightly packed rocks and trees, catching her when she started to stagger and fall, she was unable to tackle it. She collapsed before they reached the top of the landslide that blocked their way, sinking to her knees with a mirthless little laugh.

"I can't, Sam. I'm sorry, but I just can't. You go on. There's no sense in both of us dying out here."

"Nobody is dying," he said fiercely. "Got that?"

"Yes, but—"

"No more talking. That's an official order."

According to her, he was an FBI agent, so the command he'd just issued seemed appropriate. To his relief, she voiced no further objection, not even when he crouched down beside her, gathered her up in his arms and rose to his feet.

What with the bulky parka she wore and the cumbersome bag over her shoulder, not to mention her thick boots, he expected her weight to be a challenge for him. But somehow, even though he had to climb with her to the crest of the landslide, she didn't seem like a burden. Maybe just because he liked the way she felt in his arms, her face nestled against his chest, her arms wrapped around his neck.

Still, he was thankful when he reached the summit, where he stopped to fill his lungs with air. The curtain of snow that had eased long enough to reveal the origin of the landslide had lifted altogether. From this height, he had a clear view of what lay below them on the other side of the barrier. And it was not more of the same.

Only yards away from the foot of the landslide, the river widened, spreading out into a frozen lake rimmed by forest. To Sam's further amazement, he could make out a small clearing off the shore less than a mile away. Not a vacant clearing either. There was a log cabin there beneath a canopy of pines.

A miracle? Or the mirage Eve had talked about earlier? It was hard to tell through the haze of flakes that were falling again. If he had to choose, though—and he did—he was going to believe in the reality of that cabin.

"Can you see it, Eve? There's a cabin out there on the lake! The shelter we've been praying for!"

Her only reply was a long sigh. If this was all she was capable of, then it was imperative that they reach that cabin as quickly as possible.

Carrying his precious cargo, and with no further hesitation, Sam picked his way carefully down the rough, treacherous slope. The going should have been easier when he reached the bottom and was able to strike out across the level ice. It wasn't.

The wind on the river had been bad enough, but out here on the open lake it was ferocious, made worse by the snow that had descended in force again, stinging their faces like needles of ice. A snow that obscured all sight of the cabin in the clearing.

He couldn't afford to make any mistake and miss that clearing, which was why he hugged the shoreline, even if a direct route across the lake would have been faster. Nor was he willing to trust the ice over deeper waters where the crust might not be thick enough to support them.

"Sam?"

Another blessing. Hearing her voice meant she was still with him. "What is it?"

"Can I talk now?"

Her request had him chuckling. "Yes, you can talk now."

"Then what I want to say is, you should put me down. I can walk again. I'm rested, and I must be too heavy for you to go on carrying me like this."

"Just stay where you are."

That she didn't argue with him about it meant she hadn't recovered her strength. Besides, crazy though it might be under the circumstances, he continued to enjoy the sensation of her in his arms, the way she felt all soft and compliant and trusting against him.

He even liked the sound of her voice when she started to babble again.

"I really am a good cook, Sam…I'll show you what a good cook I am…if I can get my hands on a stove and some ingredients…do you suppose there will be food in the cabin, Sam?…I hope there will be food of some kind…"

"Me, too, angel. Me, too."

Not until they reached the edge of the clearing did

Sam notice there was a small building down on the shore. Probably a boatshed of some kind. He spared it no more than a quick glance. He was interested in nothing but the log cabin itself situated above them under the tall pines.

The slope was an easy one to ascend, permitting him to examine the structure as he headed toward it, Eve still in his arms. Its windows were shuttered, meaning it couldn't be occupied. He figured it must be an isolated fishing cabin used only in the warmer months. There was certainly no sign of anyone here now.

Steps mounted to a covered porch stretched across the face of the cabin. There was a generous supply of firewood stacked against the wall and a bench beside the front door. Only when he lowered Eve, placing her gently on the bench, did Sam realize his arms ached from having borne her up that ridge and around the lake, all the while battling his way through the glacial wind.

Didn't matter. All that counted was getting them inside and getting a fire going. The wood here was evidence that a fire was possible. They both needed the warmth of a healthy blaze, Eve in particular. She was silent now, having talked herself out long before they reached the clearing. Not a good sign.

"I'm going to leave you here, but only long enough to find a way to get us inside. Okay?"

She nodded, sagging against the log wall behind her. He hated leaving her, even for a few essential minutes, but at least she was out of the wind.

The front door, a solid barrier, was locked when he tried it. He might have known that entry wouldn't be easy. No choice but to find another way in.

Leaving the shelter of the porch, he worked his way around the side of the cabin, folding back the hinged shutters as he went. The windows, too, were all securely fastened from the inside. Not that he wouldn't hesitate to break a pane to get at one of those locks, but only if it proved necessary.

He had much better luck at the rear of the cabin. There was another, smaller porch here, and when he tried the back door it rattled in its frame. All it needed to force it was his shoulder thrust hard and repeatedly against its planks. With one final, mighty shove the door burst open.

Hallelujah, he was inside!

Although his effort had damaged the lock and the latch, the door itself was still intact, enabling him to close it behind him and keep it shut by propping a chair under its knob.

He was in a small kitchen. Off to one side were open shelves. As poor as the light was, he could make out some glass jars that looked like they contained a variety of dried foodstuffs. Things like rice and beans. Thank God they wouldn't starve.

He wasted no time in inspecting either the layout of the cabin or its furnishings, noting only there was a stone fireplace as he strode rapidly through the dim interior to the front door, which he unlocked and opened.

Eve hadn't moved from the bench. Her eyes were closed now, which was all he needed to tell him how urgent it was that he get her inside and warm. Scooping her up into his arms, he carried her into the cabin, kicking the door shut behind them.

There was an easy chair in a corner of the living room. She stirred when Sam placed her on it, then was still again. Turning away, he crossed to the fireplace. A large basket loaded with wood sat at the side of the hearth. He wouldn't have to use its contents until later on, since a fire had already been laid in the grate, requiring nothing but a match. There was a box of matches on the mantel.

He hesitated. A fire meant smoke streaming from the chimney. Smoke that could be spotted by the enemy. But not in this weather, when the snowfall outside was heavy enough to obscure it, when the afternoon was already beginning to darken. Nor was that chopper likely to be in the air in these conditions. For Eve's sake, he persuaded himself to risk it.

Box in hand, he hunkered down on the hearth, opened the damper, lit one of the long matches and touched its flame to the kindling under the split logs. Only when he was satisfied that he had a good fire under way did Sam turn his attention again to Eve.

He realized it would take some time for even a strong blaze to warm the room. He had to get her close to the fireplace, preferably stretched out on the floor so she would get the full benefit of its heat. But first—

Getting to his feet, Sam did a rapid survey of their surroundings. The cabin was small. Weak though the light was, he didn't need a tour of it to understand its simple arrangement. Living room here, the kitchen behind it and a couple of bedrooms off to the side, all of them plainly furnished.

It was the bedrooms he wanted. There were two sets of bunk beds in one of them and a pair of twin beds in the other, all of them stripped down to their mattresses. Helping himself to one of those mattresses, he dragged it into the living room where he placed it near the hearth. Eve's eyes remained closed when he laid her on the mattress. She seemed to be breathing normally, however. He felt he could leave her again for another few minutes.

Water. They would both need water. And food. But that would have to wait.

He went into the kitchen where there was a stove for cooking and kerosene lamps ranged along a counter. No electricity, naturally, and no running water, either. The sink was a dry one, the only source of water a hand pump out in the yard. He'd noticed it earlier when he'd rounded the back of the cabin. But it wouldn't be active at this time of the year.

They would have to depend on melted snow.

Finding a clean, plastic bucket in one of the cupboards under the counter, he went outside and packed it with snow. He could make out a tiny structure a short distance away under the trees. He figured it was a privy. Without a bathroom in the cabin, they would have to depend on that, too.

All the comforts of home. If your home resembled nothing more than a pioneer cabin, that is.

What are you complaining about, McDonough? Primitive or otherwise, this place is the haven you prayed for.

No way of knowing who the absent owners of the place were. He'd spotted a framed photograph on one of the walls in the living room. Two middle-aged guys with their fishing gear, proudly displaying their catches. They looked enough alike to be brothers, and possibly were. Could be the owners. Whoever did own the cabin, he blessed them for its existence.

Snow-filled bucket in hand, he went back inside and placed it near the hearth. It would take a while for the snow to melt. But the snow Eve had collected on her clothes during their trek had already melted. She must be wet clean through. Hell, even with the warmth of the fire, asleep or not, she would soon be shivering.

His own clothes were wet, as well. The obvious solution was for him to get both of them undressed and under a pair of warm blankets. Returning to the room with the twin beds, he hauled the other mattress out to the living room and placed it next to the first mattress.

A second visit to the bedroom produced a couple of blankets, which he tossed down on the empty mattress. The living room was warm enough now that he could afford to peel off his coat. After shedding the rest, his boots, gloves and earmuffs, he knelt down on the rug beside Eve and began to remove her damp garments.

His action was a necessity. There should have been nothing erotic about it. Yeah, and randy bastard that he was, he shouldn't be getting all hot and bothered with each article of clothing he stripped away from her sensational body.

He couldn't help it. She was so tempting lying there, such an irresistible woman, that he couldn't keep himself from wanting her. The worst of it was, she never opened her eyes, never seemed in any way aware of his efforts. Damn, he was taking advantage of her.

Another thought struck him then. Maybe she wasn't just sleeping. Maybe he should be worried about her state of unconsciousness. Which meant he ought to feel nothing but relief when, seconds later, his act of rolling her slacks down her long, shapely legs finally roused her. Well, he was relieved. But he also suffered a quick pang of guilt. She had caught him.

In the long moment that followed, her wide, green eyes searching his, the only sound in the room was the crackle of the wood burning on the grate. There was nothing accusing in her gaze, or in her voice when she got around to speaking to him softly.

"Are you seducing me, Sam?"

His own voice was raspy when he answered her with a slow "I'm trying hard not to, angel."

"That's too bad, but only sensible, I suppose. I do want you to make love to me, Sam, but right now I'm so tired

I'm afraid I'd be asleep again before you could get in the first kiss."

It was definitely arousing that she was letting him know without shyness that she desired him as much as he desired her. But, as she'd pointed out, not sensible.

"We'll wait," he reluctantly assured her.

"I promise to do better next time." Her eyes closed. With a little sigh, she drifted off to sleep again.

He didn't try to take off her panties and bra, which were all that remained on her body when he covered her with one of the blankets. He could endure only so much temptation.

He was exhausted himself. Too exhausted to even think about that food in the kitchen. That, also, would have to wait a bit.

Adding wood to the fire, he peeled off his own wet clothes down to the skin, stretched himself out on the other mattress and drew the second blanket over him.

Though there were only a few inches separating him from Eve, he managed to resist any contact with her. It was the only way he could will himself to sleep.

Chapter 5

Eve came awake with a start to a multitude of eyes staring down at her. Eyes that gleamed like glass in the softly flickering firelight.

That, she realized, after a few seconds of staring back at them, was probably because they *were* glass. Or whatever material the taxidermist had used.

The trophies were mounted on the log walls all around the room. Fish mostly, possibly caught right here in the lake out front, but there were also the heads of two deer.

Eve found them a little intimidating, maybe because of the shadows in the room. The only illumination came from the dwindling fire, unless you counted the fast-fading twilight framed in the window across from her.

She must have slept away what had remained of the afternoon after their arrival at the cabin. Enough hours anyway that her body felt restored. And now it was almost night, and she was thirsty. *Very* thirsty, not to mention hollow with hunger.

Water was her priority, however, which was why she propped herself up on one elbow in an initial effort to determine just where she might find it. The liquid version, that is, because there was all that snow outside. It had satisfied them until now, and if it was necessary she could—

Eve got no further than that. Her sudden discovery of the sleeping figure on the mattress adjoining her own stopped her where she was. The sight of him had her catching her breath. Talk about intimidating!

Apparently, without his being aware of it, the blanket covering Sam had worked its way down to his waist. Or possibly, if the heat of the fire had made him too warm, it had been a conscious, deliberate action. Whatever the explanation, he was now naked from the waist up. And maybe just as entirely naked below that.

Not that she needed to imagine what was still under the blanket. What was above it was satisfying enough. Wide shoulders with the tattoo of a dragon wrapped around the biceps of one arm, a powerful chest lightly dusted with dark, curling hair and that hair arrowing down in a thin line to the promise of a flat abdomen. Whatever existence this man had lived before his memory loss, it must have included regular workouts to produce a raw, wholly masculine sexuality like this.

Eve interrupted her visual pleasure with the sudden realization that she was as nude as he was under her blanket. Or would be, if Sam hadn't spared her her bra and panties. She had a vague recollection of his having stripped her of her wet clothes.

And this voyeurism, she told herself sharply, had gone

far enough. She needed that water, and Sam would, too, when he awakened.

It wasn't until she climbed to her feet, hugging the blanket around her tightly, that she saw the bucket of what was likely melted snow on the hearth. Sam again. It was time she made her own effort on their behalf.

She'd need a glass or a cup to dip water out of the bucket. The kitchen, or what passed for a kitchen in the cabin, would furnish that. And maybe, if she were very lucky, something that would keep them from starving.

Eve supposed that the room behind the living room was the kitchen. The light was so weak when she entered the area it was hard to tell. Only when she smacked into what turned out to be a cooking stove was she sure this was the kitchen. Groping her way around the stove, she reached a wall of cupboards. Her fingers felt dishes when she opened the first door. There was something else on the shelf. A box which might, or might not, contain food.

The kitchen was like a freezer, not at all conducive to any further investigation. Taking the box, along with a mug, she returned to the living room. It had chilled in her absence. The fire needed building up.

Placing the box and the mug on the mantel, she fueled the fire with wood from the basket before dipping the mug into the bucket. Then, with the box tucked under her arm, one hand gripping the mug and the other managing to hang on to her blanket, she settled cross-legged on her mattress.

Her first order of business was to check on Sam. A quick glance told her he was still peacefully asleep on his own mattress. Only then was she ready to satisfy her thirst.

Whatever the taste of the melted snow, she swallowed it gratefully while examining the box she'd transferred to her lap. The firelight informed her she had discovered a treasure. If the label was correct, the box contained sealed packages of saltine crackers!

The snapping of the burning wood on the grate had no effect on Sam. But the sound of her fingers eagerly ripping open one of those packages did. He sat up so suddenly his blanket slid even further down his body, threatening to reveal much more than his sleekly muscled, lip-licking chest.

Eve Warren, you are an absolute wanton as far as this man is concerned. You know that, don't you?

Yeah, she did know it, which is why she lifted her gaze to his puzzled face, informing him quickly, "Crackers, Sam. I found crackers in the kitchen and a mug. Here, there's still water in it, if you don't mind drinking after me."

He accepted the mug she held out to him with a slow, husky response that had her stomach doing flip-flops. "Angel, I'd love to put my mouth where your lips have been."

He gulped from the mug. Eve was gulping herself. Only hers were dry gulps as she watched the way his Adam's apple bobbed as he swallowed the water.

Was her interest that obvious? Was that why, when he lowered the mug, he asked her a simple "What?"

He'd caught her staring at him. She tried to correct what had plainly been a sexual fascination with a hopefully playful "Did you know you have a dragon on your arm? No, the other arm."

He looked down at the dragon curling around his biceps. "So I do."

Considering he hadn't been out of his clothes since his memory loss—until now, that is—his surprise at the existence of a tattoo was understandable.

"I was just wondering if there was a story connected to it," she said in a lame effort to maintain her innocence.

"Could be. I'll have one of those crackers now, please."

The next few moments were devoted to sitting there on their mattresses passing the box and the mug, which Sam refilled, back and forth to each other. At any other time the plain crackers they munched on would have held little interest for Eve. But in her present state of hunger they were as filling as a feast.

Between bites and sips, she found the courage to ask him, "I said some pretty crazy things out there on the ice, didn't I?"

She had no clear recollection of exactly what those things were. She did, however, vividly remember just how warm and secure she had felt in his arms. But that was something she wasn't ready to admit.

"I seem to recall," he said with a teasing grin, "the promise of a fabulous meal once you got your hands on a stove and the right ingredients."

"If all there is in that kitchen are crackers, *fabulous* it won't be."

"I noticed other stuff. But whatever you fix when you get around to it, I won't complain. Anyway," he went on, his voice deepening, "I found what you had to say while I was stripping away your wet clothes more interesting. *Much* more interesting."

When his unmistakably intimate gaze focused on her with those suddenly slumberous eyes, Eve felt like a butterfly who has just been pinned. Clearing her throat, she managed a quick "About that…"

"So you do remember *that* promise?"

"I— Yes, I remember."

She could feel his body heat as he shifted closer to her, making her woozy with an undeniable longing. "You are aware that I stripped away my own wet clothes, *all* of them, before I crawled under this blanket?"

"I can see that."

"Uh-huh. Then, since we're no longer either thirsty or hungry, and since you're almost entirely naked yourself, I'd say this was the perfect time and place to make good on that promise."

She put down the box of crackers currently in her possession. "Satisfy another need, you mean?"

He put down the mug in his own possession. "I can't think of any reason not to. Can you?"

She could, had she permitted herself to address the consequences of their action when his memory returned. But, reckless or not, in this moment she wanted him too badly for that. "Not a single one," she agreed, shedding any last remnants of restraint.

Whatever regrets might surface, she would count them later. Right now all she cared about was Sam's mouth, which settled on her own. Lightly at first, his teeth and the tip of his tongue experimenting gently with her lips, carefully nipping and bathing them.

He was in no hurry. He must be thinking they had all night for this. Good for him, because she wanted to savor everything he had to offer her. And she did. The sensation of his firm lips tugging on her, the masculine scent that could only be his, his warm breath mingling with her own as they inhaled each other.

His patience was a virtue. Hers, she decided in the end, was nonexistent. He had to have sensed she was ready for more. That had to be why he began to kiss her. And, oh, how this man could kiss! With all the skill and concentration at his command, his lips branded hers before his tongue slid into her mouth, seeking and finding her flavor, inviting her to taste him in return. Eve did just that, her tongue searching for his, mating with it.

She was moaning with pleasure long before he intensified his kiss with a fierceness so vital it seemed to reach her deepest emotions, lifting them to heights beyond her description. Those emotions so occupied her that Eve was never conscious of just when and how he removed the blanket from around her, unclasped her bra and cast it aside.

Awareness returned to her in a rush only when, drawing back from her, his gaze molten, he uttered a slow, husky "They're beautiful, sweetheart. Your breasts are as beautiful as the rest of you. They make me want to—"

"What, Sam? Show me what you want to do with them," she whispered, shocked by her boldness.

Or maybe not. Maybe in this moment *shocked* wasn't in her vocabulary. Not when, obeying her invitation, he didn't hesitate to take possession of her breasts, his big hands cupping their fullness, thumbs stroking her tender flesh. His mouth followed, accompanied by his low groans as he tasted and teased her nipples, in turn, until they were hard buds of pure yearning.

"No more," she pleaded, unable to endure the torment he was inflicting on her.

"It's not enough," he said harshly, lifting his face from her swollen breasts. "Not nearly enough."

Clasping her hands, he carried them to his chest where he treated her to another form of torture. And himself, as well, if the sound of him sharply sucking in his breath was any indication as she flattened her palms against slabs of hard muscle, her fingers sifting through his chest hair, following the trail down to a quivering stomach and beyond to—

She paused in sudden wonder. When had he shoved

aside the rest of his blanket to complete the exposure of his fully naked body in all its raw, riveting masculinity? A sight at whose center proudly rose his arousal. Unable to resist the temptation, Eve's hand closed around the hot, throbbing shaft that was both steel and silk.

"Now, Sam? Is *now* enough?"

"Sweet heaven," he gasped, "you're killing me."

"Then show me what dying is."

He obliged her by pressing her down against her mattress, which he now shared, by swiftly removing her panties to bury his face between her parted thighs. Before she could object, or wanted to object, that expert tongue of his was busy again, probing the core of her being.

Clutching his head, she dug her fingers into his scalp when he centered his attention on her wet nub, working his magic until she was lost in a frenzy of passion. A passion so strong he had to grip her squirming hips to prevent her from escaping his focus. He gave her no relief, lifting her steadily, relentlessly to a peak of such giddy joy she lost all control, surrendering herself in the end with whimpers and little cries to wave after wave of blissful release.

He owned her now. She was his. It's what Eve felt as she sank back to earth. That and, along with it, the belief she'd be permitted an interval of recovery. She was mistaken. Sam wasn't ready to allow either her or himself any moment of rest.

Puzzled, she watched him move quickly and with purpose away from her on hands and knees, affording her a view of a nude, supremely sexy backside.

"Sam, what are you—?"

"Shh," he hushed her.

Reaching one of the chairs over which he had earlier draped his clothing, he snagged the coat down, fumbled in one of its pockets and removed something she wasn't able to identify in the weak light of the fire. Not, anyway, until he returned to the mattress.

"Courtesy of Ken Redfeather," he said, holding out a foil-wrapped condom to her.

And just when, she wondered, had he discovered this particular treasure? He gave her no chance to question him about it. Grinning, all he would confess was a fast "There are others in that pocket—a nice supply of them."

"I take it we're not through here then?"

"Not unless you want us to be."

"I wouldn't do that to either of us, Sam," she said, accepting the packet he pressed on her after he tore it open.

"You do the honors."

There was no mistaking his invitation. He wanted her to sheathe him, an action that her limited experience hadn't prepared her for. His fully evident erection was all the assistance he was willing to provide her.

And, as it turned out, all she needed to convince her of the power of her womanhood was when he trembled visibly as she removed the condom and slowly rolled it down over his pulsing column of rigid flesh.

"You're destroying me again," he accused her.

Maybe so, but it didn't prevent him from taking over after that. Establishing his own male power, his hands urging her down again on the mattress, he lifted himself above her, nudged her legs open with his knee and lowered himself on her flushed body.

Too plainly wanting her by now to sacrifice even a moment of delay, he gave her no chance to accept him before guiding himself to the entrance he sought. Eve made every effort to accommodate him, spreading her legs, lifting her hips to receive the tip of his erection that slowly, steadily parted the folds of the slick, quivering flesh that waited for him so impatiently.

She must have somehow silently communicated her readiness to welcome him, because with one strong thrust that had her gasping, he plunged his length deep inside her. Only then did he pause to allow her to adjust to him. To relish the incredible sensation of his body joined with hers.

In that sweet interval he began to kiss her again, his open mouth demonstrating his intense passion, tongue delving into her mouth to capture her own tongue in a duel of pure, potent sensation.

In the end, the shared urgency of a lower, more demanding region of their locked bodies would no longer deny either of them the fury that followed. Sam's long strokes which, with her legs and arms wrapped about him she strove to match with her own rhythms, were dynamic. They were accompanied by his murmured endearments and wild kisses that she answered with her hands and mouth on every portion of his sleek flesh that she could reach.

Surging against each other, both of them beyond control now, she felt the first spasms break over her, sweeping her into the flood that carried her away.

She was just surfacing when Sam was seized by his own climax and a dark, muttered claim that she had drowned him. If so, he went with a smile and a sigh of satisfaction as he sank against her.

When he stirred again, it was with a concerned "I'm too heavy for you."

Before she could assure him he wasn't, that she wanted him to remain exactly where he was, he rolled away from her on his side.

"Turn over. No, the other direction," he instructed her

when she started to face him. She did as he asked, her back to him. "There, that's better. Just right."

He squeezed against her, his arms sliding around her waist to lock her in his protective embrace. Yes, this *was* just right, their bodies spooned together so snugly she could feel his breath stirring in her hair. Could hear his whisper in her ear.

"What just happened...that was fantastic. *You're* fantastic."

"Without a memory," she murmured, "how can you compare?"

"I know. On some level way down inside me, I know. Here—" Removing one of his hands from her waist, he reached for a blanket, drawing it over them, sealing them in a warm, safe cocoon.

She listened to the soft sputtering of the fire, felt him relax against her and knew from his even breathing that he had drifted off. Eve wasn't ready to sleep.

In the long minutes that followed, she wanted nothing more than to remain peacefully suspended in the pleasure this remarkable man had given her. She didn't want to think about any negatives, but they came crowding in on her anyway, demanding her attention.

Somewhere in the wilderness outside this cabin was the threat of the enemy hunting for them. The wind that still howled under the eaves reminded her of that. It should have been her chief concern. It wasn't. It was Sam who worried her. How would he feel about her when his memory returned? How fantastic would he think she was then?

And how would she feel about him? How did she feel about him *now?* Vulnerable, that's how she felt. Fearing that, if she tried to get in touch with her emotions, *hon-*

estly tried, she could be laying herself open to some serious hurt.

Did she regret their lovemaking? It had occurred to her before she had given herself to him so freely that she might. No, she decided. Whatever happened after tonight, she had no regrets for what they had so wonderfully shared. Not a single one.

Then why was she so scared?

Chapter 6

Sam wondered if he had ever been in the service. Maybe that's why the voice rousing him from his pleasant state of sleep reminded him of a tough drill sergeant, demanding that he get out of bed.

"Come on, Sam, it's time for you to be up."

Naw, couldn't be a drill sergeant. This voice, insistent though it was, had the velvet tone of a woman. Opening one eye, he checked to make certain of that. Yep, the figure bending over him was definitely female, and a mighty alluring one at that.

"You're dressed already," he said.

"I have been for quite a while," Eve informed him.

"What time is—" He didn't finish his question. Having propped himself up on one elbow, he realized there was no need for him to ask. Gray daylight framing the cabin windows told him it was morning. "My God, we must have slept the clock around!"

"And then some. We probably needed it."

From the way she was hovering over him so expectantly, Sam guessed there was going to be no early morning, drowsy snuggling followed by another session of lovemaking. Damn!

"What have you been doing?"

"Keeping busy."

She began to hand him his clothes, garment by garment, her intention clear. She wanted him to get into them. At least they were thoroughly dry by now. Thanks to her. Hell, she must have been keeping the fire going right through the night.

The fire!

Damning himself for his negligence, he swiveled his gaze in the direction of the fireplace where smoke from the burning logs was being drawn up the chimney.

"Eve, no. We have to put it out. No fire, not in daylight. The smoke could be seen for miles."

"Sam, I didn't overlook that problem. But it's not. A problem, that is. You know how crazy April can be."

"Angel, what are you talking about?"

"The weather. The snow and wind quit sometime in the night, probably hours ago. And after that the temperature had to have climbed. Climbed a lot, because right now there's nothing out there but a very thick fog."

He understood then what she was telling him. The fog was swallowing their smoke, blending it into the gray mass that must have blanketed the entire area. But Sam wouldn't be satisfied until he saw it for himself.

Surging to his feet, hopping from one foot to the other as he struggled first into his briefs and then his pants, he worked his way to the nearest window. She was right. The fog was so heavy it shrouded the lake below from sight, cloaked the cabin, concealing it and any smoke from both the ground and the air above.

"We're all right then," he said, turning from the window.

"But at the first sign of the fog lifting—"

"We extinguish the fire."

Able to relax his guard, at least for the moment, he became aware of the aroma of brewing coffee. The smell of it was so irresistible Sam was ready to forgive her for being dressed when he'd wanted her to be naked and close beside him on the mattress.

"Coffee?" he wondered. "Actual coffee?"

"Much more than that," she said, her tone registering her excitement. "We won't have to exist on crackers."

The promise of food in any form was also an enticement. But first he had something more important to take care of.

Fully dressed now and coat in hand, he headed for the back door and that privy he had spotted last evening. Eve must have already visited the place. Once outside and bundling into his coat, he could see her tracks in the snow.

It wasn't until he came away from the privy that Sam made himself fully aware of the weather. The dense fog was in their favor. If the enemy was aloft again in that chopper, they wouldn't be able to spot anything below them.

That wasn't the only good sign. The air was so mild he could swear the snowdrifts were already drooping. A total change from yesterday. It was no guarantee the temperature would continue to climb. As Eve had pointed out, April was a month that couldn't decide what it wanted to be. But maybe…

Not wanting to jinx his hope for a quick thaw that

might aid them in getting away, he didn't finish the thought.

Eve was in the kitchen stirring a pot of something on the woodstove when he returned to the cabin. She looked as cheerful as if she'd realized that ambition of hers to be a chef.

That she'd managed to build a fire in the stove and had a basin of water waiting for him on the dry sink, evidence she also had melted a quantity of snow, had him feeling guilty. Just how long had she been up and about without him? he wondered, sliding the chair back under the knob of the damaged back door.

She handed him a towel after he'd washed his hands and face with a bar of soap.

"I found an unopened toothbrush along with the soap," she told him as he dried himself. "Just the one, so we'll have to share it."

Not a problem, he thought, considering how intimate their mouths had been last night.

"There's a package of disposable razors, too."

Good. No more risk of whisker burns when he kissed her again, which he fully intended to do as soon as possible. Right now, though, his hunger was a priority.

"What have you got cooking in the pot?"

"Oatmeal. We'll have scrambled eggs to go with it. Powdered, of course, like the milk that gets mixed in with the eggs, so I don't know how they'll taste. But, Sam, you wouldn't believe what we've lucked into here."

She began pulling open drawers and cupboard doors, showing him tightly sealed containers of flour, sugar, a variety of dried meats and fruits and an assortment of seasonings. There were also the jars of rice and beans he'd noticed yesterday on the open shelves.

"Everything is nonperishable, which I guess it has to be without a refrigerator."

Sam nodded. "Well, whoever the owners of this isolated place are, groceries must be a problem if they have to be hauled in with them from any distance, probably either by boat along the river or maybe a floatplane out on the lake." He tossed the towel down on the counter. "You happen to come across any tools?"

"In the drawer over there."

Great. At least he could make an effort to repair the latch and lock on the back door, saving them from the nuisance of using the chair to keep the door shut. As much as he admired Eve's resourcefulness, along with a growing list of other qualities about this amazing woman, he had been feeling pretty useless since she had awakened him. He'd need to remedy that.

She had breakfast ready and waiting on the table when he successfully finished with the door. "Not bad," he complimented her after tasting the eggs. "Not bad at all."

"It's the spices that save them."

"Whatever the secret, you are one hell of a cook, Eve Warren. That restaurant you're planning to open will definitely be a hit."

Sam could see he had pleased her, and that made him feel good. For the moment, anyway. He hated the thought of having to spoil her enthusiasm, but before they finished their breakfast it would be necessary for him to do just that.

"Only with the right ingredients and a restaurant-size range to cook on. One that doesn't qualify as a museum piece and has to be fueled by wood. Although," she said, glancing at the ancient iron cookstove, "I'm not a stranger to this kind of antique."

She went on to tell him that, while researching an article for the magazine on how their ancestors prepared meals for their families, she'd had the opportunity to use such a cookstove at a re-created pioneer village outside St. Louis.

It was an interesting anecdote, but Sam only half listened to it. The other half of his mind dealt with the reality that had been gnawing at him at a gut level from the moment he had opened his eyes this morning.

In the end it was Eve who, finally aware of his silence, gave him the opening he needed. "What is it, Sam? What's bothering you?"

Lowering the mug of coffee he'd been sipping from, he leaned toward her across the table, his tone one of necessary authority. "Angel, as tempting as it is, we can't go on staying here playing house."

"You're telling me we need to clear out. When?"

"As soon as the fog shows any sign of lifting. Because when it does, there's nothing to prevent our bad boys from taking to the air again in that chopper of theirs. They could already be up and searching for us."

"It's a big wilderness out there, Sam, and they can't possibly know where we went."

"Dammit, Eve, it isn't safe for us here."

"And just where do we go that *will* make us safe?"

"Downriver. Sooner or later, we're bound to reach some kind of settlement that will put us in touch with the outside world."

"They could just as well find us there or on the river itself while we're trying to get to this settlement you're counting on."

"We are not going to sit around waiting for them," he insisted.

She gazed at him solemnly for a few seconds before nodding slowly. "You're right, of course. We'll go as soon as the fog starts to thin." She got to her feet and began to clear the table. "But until then…"

"Until then, what?"

"I'm going to use the time to put food and water together for the trek."

He could see that made sense. To go out there again without the essentials would be courting suicide. He hesitated before asking her, "You mind taking care of that end of it?"

He went on to explain that he felt the need to go down to the shore, where he would try to learn if there *was* a downriver or whether the stream ended on the lake. He also meant to check the ice to make certain it was still solid. And while he was there, he would look through the boatshed for anything that might be useful to them. Not to mention being on the alert for any sign of the enemy.

Sam had been pleased by the rising temperature when he'd come away from the privy earlier. But when he emerged from the cabin again and stood on the front porch, listening to the drip of water from the melting snow on the roof, he began to regret that development.

He should have realized that a thaw wouldn't benefit them. That if it got any warmer the ice downstream might not remain reliable enough to bear them. Providing, that is, such a route existed at all. Yesterday, in the heavy snowfall, he hadn't been able to make out the end of the lake, and with this fog today it was still hidden from him. But since the river entered the lake, it only made sense that there would be an outlet somewhere out there.

Leaving the porch, he made his way down the slope in the direction of the shore, pausing at intervals to listen for the sound of any aircraft. Nothing. There was only the eerie silence of the motionless fog, its dampness licking at his face. He could almost smell it.

However, the ice concerned him when he reached the shoreline. He could neither see nor hear any open waters flowing yet on the lake. Didn't mean the cover was still safe. He needed to test it.

Moving with care, he ventured out several yards on the lake, risking a plunge through the surface when he stomped his boot on the snow-crusted ice. There was no give in any of the spots he tried. The ice was still hard and secure.

Still, he couldn't convince himself a massive thaw wasn't imminent, and if they were caught by an ice breakup while on the river... Yeah, that would be bad. Even worse, the fickle weather could trap them in another blizzard, and this time with no handy shelter.

Hell, there were no good options, were there?

Might as well investigate that boatshed while he was here. Perhaps it would provide him with some kind of weapon to use to defend them if, and when, they encountered their pursuers again at close range.

Circling the structure, he discovered that it had no windows. There were two wide doors, however, one on the water side and the other facing the cabin.

He didn't have to force any entry this time. The waterside door he tried was unlocked. He left it open for light when he went inside. The first thing he noticed was a lightweight, fiberglass canoe. When the fog finally cleared, and there was an ice breakup, the canoe could carry them downriver.

Maybe. All these *maybes*.

Other than an assortment of fishing gear, there was little else of interest in the shed. Certainly no weapons of any kind. Not so much as a bow and arrows. There were no firearms in the cabin, either—nothing like a hunting rifle. He'd already looked for one earlier. The owners would probably have taken that kind of thing with them.

Shutting the shed door behind him, he returned to the cabin where he found Eve in the kitchen assembling the last of the provisions they would take with them down-river.

"I found these in one of the cupboards," she said, indicating two plastic, capped bottles on the counter that she had already filled with water. "As for food, there's beef jerky over here, along with some dried fruits and nuts. I figured we would divide the stuff, maybe carry the loads in backpacks we might be able to fashion out of a pair of blankets. We'll need blankets if we have to spend another night in the open."

Sam gazed at her, moved by the spirit in her voice. There was an enemy somewhere out there, just waiting for the opportunity to find them again. Eve knew that, knew it just as well as he did. And yet she was handling that certainty with a courage that tugged at his gut.

Despite the insanity of it, it was there inside him. The longing to tell her how much she had already come to matter to him in these few days. How he had this strong desire not just to make love to her every time she came near him but to hold her close, emotionally as well as physically. To keep her safe. To make her his own.

It would be reckless of him, however, to express such feelings. As long as he had this memory loss, with no past and no real identity, he couldn't let himself get deeply serious about her. The trouble was, he already cared about her far too much.

But until he fully regained his memory, knew just what he had to offer her, any commitment would be unfair to both of them. And so far, except for disjointed fragments here and there that didn't always make sense to him, he wasn't much closer to finding that memory. In Sam's opinion, it made him less than a whole man.

It was after he told her what he'd learned down at the lake, then shaved and brushed his teeth, that Eve sought his opinion about fixing lunch for them.

"With the fog out there showing no sign of any letup, I think it would still be safe to use the stove. It wouldn't take me long to put together something with the noodles and dried beef. We ought to have one last, hot nourishing meal before we leave here," she reasoned. "There's no telling when we'll be able to eat like that again."

Her argument was sound. As long as they were prepared to douse their fires at the first indication the fog might be thinning, Sam had no objection to her plan.

He left her in the kitchen working her culinary magic and went outside to haul in more wood. With two fires to feed, they were burning up a considerable amount of fuel. It might even be necessary to split more logs. There was no shortage of them on the back porch.

Locating an axe in a cupboard beside the fireplace, he went outside, found a spot to work and began to cleave the logs that hadn't already been split and stacked on the front porch.

The labor was a welcome outlet for his restless energy. More than that, it gave him the opportunity to work on his memory. It was probably something that couldn't be summoned at will, but to his satisfaction he was able to achieve just that.

Still pieces, nothing complete, but it was enough. By the time he had a pile of split wood ready to carry into the cabin, he'd been able to recall images of his rigorous FBI training sessions at Quantico. He even remembered the other rooms in his Chicago apartment and his squad supervisor at headquarters. But not all the rest. Not yet.

Although he made an effort to restrain his excitement, Sam must have had a look on his face that betrayed him. Because when Eve finally called him into lunch, she gazed at him thoughtfully, maybe wondering whether he'd made any progress in regaining his memory. She didn't question him, however, and he appreciated that. He wasn't ready to tell her, not until he'd recovered the rest.

They talked instead about the meal she had waiting for them on the table. After a few bites, he praised the steaming beef and noodles.

"I guess it's good enough," she agreed.

"You underestimate yourself. It's better than just good."

This time he helped her with the cleanup when they rose from the table.

"I should check that ice again on the lake," he told her, hanging the dish towel on its hook.

Eve didn't object. She seemed to sense he needed to be alone, not just to test the ice again but to do battle with those portions of his memory that still eluded him.

The fog remained as dense as ever, but the temperature had continued to climb. Climbed considerably. In just the relatively brief span of time Sam had been in the kitchen with Eve, there had been changes.

He could see those changes when he made his way down the hill to the lake. There were already some bare patches on the ground, along with little rivulets of melted snow trickling down the slope to join the lake.

The conditions on the lake itself were more startling. Obvious even through the fog were open spots where the water below had worked its way above the swiftly rotting ice. A breakup was already under way, needing only a stiff wind sweeping over the lake to carry the ice through whatever outlet existed on the other end.

But even without a wind, neither the lake nor that stream beyond it would be safe to travel on foot. The canoe would be their best means of getting out of here, provided that breakup occurred. If not, their only choice was to hike along the bank of the stream. The vegetation bordering streams in a forested area like this would be heavy, making the going tough, maybe even impossible.

Treacherous enough to undertake when you could clearly see your way, but in a thick fog… Dammit, when would this stuff lift?

The delay was unnerving him, making him as frustrated as their enemy must be, waiting wherever that chopper was to resume their search.

Wildly impatient now for results, he stood there on the shore, rocking on his heels, an idling engine ready to roar, needing only a destination.

Tomorrow, Sam fiercely promised himself. Too late today to attempt it, but first thing tomorrow, whatever the conditions were, he and Eve would go.

He was ready to return to the cabin when a soft splash out on the lake captured his attention. Had to be a fish surfacing in one of the openings, he thought. There must be plenty of fish in the lake. Probably trout and northern pike.

The likelihood triggered another memory. The image of an ice fishing shanty out on a frozen lake. A boy kneeling on the ice. The boy was him. His father and his uncle Jack were teaching him how to use an auger and a spud bar to drill a hole through the ice. Back in Michigan, where he had grown up.

Sam began to pace along the shore, reaching for other memories. They came freely this time, a tide of them streaming through an open gate. One by one, he selected the last pieces and fit them into place until the puzzle was whole again, complete.

Everything was there, settled firmly into his consciousness, including the explanation of those mysterious paintings. Paintings ranged along the walls of a Chicago art gallery, dimly lit by security lamps. There, in that midnight gallery, his anguish had been born all those long months ago. It was the one memory he didn't want.

You don't need those demons eating away at you like a cancer. You've got something else to think about.

With his memory fully restored now, he knew just what that *something* was. Eve Warren and what his squad supervisor, Frank Kowsloski, had told him about the case in Chicago. This was what demanded his immediate action.

All FBI now, Sam swung around and strode back up the hill. He could hear her moving around in the kitchen when he entered the cabin. She had left her shoulder bag in the living room. It was in plain sight, resting on the seat of a rocking chair in the corner.

This was his opportunity to search that bag, now while she remained unaware of his return. Wrong. As quiet as he was, she must have somehow sensed his presence. He had the bag open in his hands and was looking through its contents when she appeared in the kitchen doorway.

"Sam? What are you doing in my bag?"

His voice was sharper than he intended, without any inflection of guilt, when he confronted her. "Where is it? Where are you hiding it?"

Chapter 7

All along she had fought not to surrender her heart to him. And even though a portion of her still battled that outcome, she knew it was too late. That was what had frightened her last night after their lovemaking—that she'd already lost the struggle. And she had.

Go on, admit it. You went and fell in love with him, didn't you?

Or the man he had been, anyway. But that Sam McDonough no longer existed. This was the other Sam.

Eve didn't need to ask him if he had fully recovered his memory down there at the lake. She knew he had. She could hear it in the harshness of his voice, see it in the hardness of his expression as he came toward her, her bag in his hand.

There was something else she saw, this time in his eyes. A look of secret suffering. Back at the plane, before he'd regained consciousness, she had remembered and wondered about the tightness around his mouth prior to the crash. Even then it had suggested the existence of whatever it was that haunted him.

So, that discovery hadn't been her imagination, after all. It was real. As real as the daunting stranger who stood here now, waiting for her to answer him.

Eve had known Sam would eventually find himself again. Had told herself she would be prepared for this moment. She wasn't. If she felt anything at all beyond her state of numbness, it was sadness. Sadness and regret over the loss of the man who had come to mean everything to her.

Foolish, Eve. He's gone, and all you have is the cynical, overbearing Sam who returned with his memory. Better start accepting that.

"Are you going to tell me, or do I have to dump this bag out on the floor?"

She hated the accusing tone of his voice, the anger that drove it. Maintaining her silence, she went and sat down on one of the chairs, her hands folded in her lap. She wanted him to think she was calm and composed.

But maybe he knew she wasn't. That what she intended as an attitude of self-defense, a tempering of any grief, was nothing but an illusion. That the hands in her lap were cold, that inwardly she was neither calm nor composed. Maybe that's why he came and hovered over her. Because he knew she was vulnerable, that if he was persistent she would tell him what he wanted to know.

Not that she could, but he was right. She couldn't go on being silent. "I don't know what you think I'm hiding. Why don't you save both of us some time and just explain the mystery to me?" She'd meant her response to sound resentful, but it came out weary.

He, himself, registered impatience, which was exactly

what she expected. "Look, Eve, we can go on playing games, but sooner or later I'm going to get it out of you. So, why don't you just tell me?"

"I told you, I don't—"

"Yeah, yeah, you don't know what I'm talking about. Okay, have it your way." Dropping her bag on the floor, he seized another chair, swung it around and straddled it, facing her, his arms folded across the top rail as he leaned toward her. "The computer disk, the flash drive, whatever it is that Charlie Fowler gave you to protect for him. Now are you going to go on pretending you don't have it?"

"But I don't have it. Why on earth do you think I would?"

"Because it's the only logical explanation, although it took getting my memory back for me to figure it out."

"Explanation for what?"

"Why Victor DeMarco's thugs want you so badly. They'd have searched Charlie Fowler and his rental car after they killed him. When they didn't find what they wanted, they would have assumed Fowler entrusted you with it. So they came after you, either to get it or to make sure it was destroyed when they shot our plane down. Make sense?"

"That much does, yes. But if this computer disk, flash drive or whatever does exist, why is it so important? What does it contain?"

"Detailed information on years of tax cheating that could send a crime boss to prison for a long time. Or are you going to deny knowing that Charlie Fowler was Victor DeMarco's accountant?"

"I knew," she admitted.

"Now we're getting someplace."

"Are we?" Eve was still baffled. "I have yet to understand why anyone, including you, would assume Charlie handed this important evidence over to me."

Sam shrugged. "Maybe because he was desperate, somehow realized DeMarco's boys were getting close. He needed someone he could trust. You, Eve. Hell, you were living with him up in that ski chalet, weren't you?"

"And you think— What, Sam? That Charlie was my lover? You do think just that, don't you?"

"Do I have to point out the obvious?"

"Well, you're wrong." She could no longer avoid it. It was time he knew the truth. "Charlie was not my lover. He was my father."

She had expected him to look stunned by her revelation, or at least surprised. He was neither. His only reaction was to narrow his eyes in suspicion. "If you're lying to me—"

"It's the truth. Charlie was my father."

"Why am I just now learning this?"

"Because Charlie made me promise that I would never tell anyone I was his daughter, even an FBI special agent. He didn't explain it, but he must have feared I could be in danger if the wrong people ever learned I was his daughter. He was protecting me. Which," she added emphatically, "was why he would never have turned over a record of tax evasions to me in any form."

She watched Sam, hearing him draw a deep breath, then exhale it slowly. She knew by the look on his face, when he sat back in his chair, that he'd accepted what she had related to him. For now, anyway.

"If you don't have his electronic copy of those incriminating records, then where is it? He was planning to turn it over to the FBI as soon as he got back to Chicago." He gazed at her speculatively, caring about nothing now but the missing evidence needed to send a crime lord to prison. She no longer mattered to him, except as an assignment. "I don't suppose he…"

"No, he didn't tell me where it is. All he asked me to do was to visit his lawyer in Chicago after his death. I had the feeling it was in connection with his will. But if he has left me his money, I could never spend it on myself. Not when he earned it the way he did. Whatever it is, I'll give it all to charity, possibly cancer research."

Sam nodded, but she could see he wasn't interested in that. She meant no more to him now than the subject of an FBI-style interrogation. Was he always this intense, she wondered, whenever he conducted one of those interrogations? Maybe with a frown on his face like the one he was suddenly wearing.

Something must have occurred to him. That's why he bent toward her again with a gruff "Wait a minute. You told me back in the root cellar your father died when you were a teenager."

"And you think what? That I haven't told you the truth about Charlie?"

"Have you?"

"I did tell you the truth, both back in the root cellar and now. Until a couple of weeks ago, George Warren was the only father I'd ever known. He adopted me, gave me his name when I was an infant shortly after he married my mother."

"You never wondered about your biological father?"

"My mother was vague about him when I was old enough to ask. I was given the impression he'd died before I was born. I suppose she didn't want anyone, especially her daughter, knowing the man who fathered me worked for a crime lord."

"So you never knew Charlie Fowler was still alive, never had any contact with him?"

"I didn't say that. I did know he existed, did have contact with him. Of sorts."

"Want to explain that?"

Sam wasn't going to rest until he had it all. Eve gave it to him in a flat, resigned voice. "I knew him as *Uncle* Charlie. The uncle I never saw, who lived in Chicago and was always much too busy to ever visit us in St. Louis, but somehow was interested in my welfare."

"In what way?"

"Letters that an uncle might write to a niece, asking about her life. Birthday and Christmas presents that arrived regularly over the years, even a few phone calls. I have a feeling he may even have paid for my college education."

"A pretty odd setup, wasn't it?" Sam observed dryly.

Eve lifted her hands in a gesture meant to convey her own failure to completely understand the situation. "I can only imagine it was something arranged between Mom and Charlie. He could care about me, be generous to me, as long as he promised to keep his distance. Something like that."

"Uh-huh. And even after your stepfather and mother were gone, Fowler went on honoring that promise, until— What is it you said? A couple of weeks ago?"

"When Charlie phoned me and asked me to join him at the skiing village, he told me he had terminal cancer and wanted to spend a little time with me before the end. I couldn't refuse him, not when he was dying. It wasn't until I arrived that I learned from him he was my birth father."

"Did he also tell you he worked for DeMarco?"

"Yes. I wanted to hate him for that, but I couldn't. Not when he was my father. Not a man I only knew as someone kind and generous."

"I'll give him that," Sam allowed. "Along with the knowledge that Fowler was protecting you again when he insisted both of you travel separately to and from the skiing village."

Which, Eve thought, was something Special Agent McDonough would have been briefed about before he left Chicago. And now he knew it all. He was finished with her. That was evident when he scraped his chair back and got to his feet.

Sam had accepted her story, but she sensed he still didn't fully trust her. And probably never would again.

What an idiot she had been to fall in love with him against all her warnings to herself.

Face it, Eve. You lost what you never really had.

He hadn't called her "angel" at any time during this exchange. That, too, was probably something she would never hear again. Why this should suddenly occur to her she didn't know. It wasn't important. Or shouldn't be, even if her heart was aching over the realization.

It didn't surprise Eve that Sam kept his distance from her throughout the rest of the day, both emotionally and physically. It was what she'd expected.

She had no choice. She accepted his absences when he suddenly seemed to have a list of essential tasks to undertake, all of which he attacked with a nervous energy. Extinguishing the fire in the kitchen stove, burying the ashes in the snow behind the cabin, closing and fastening all the shutters outside.

He explained this last action with a brief "If the fog lifts before we have a chance to pull out of here and that chopper should come nosing around, I want them to think there's no one down here."

His one exception was the front window overlooking

the porch, where the overhang of the roof would conceal it from the air. Eve realized without being told that this one window needed to remain unshuttered in order for Sam to monitor the situation out front.

Not that there was anything he could monitor in the thick, persistent fog. Which was why at regular intervals throughout the afternoon he visited the lake below to check the condition of the ice. Of course, those frequent visits could also be an excuse to avoid her. Not that Eve questioned him about them, fearing it would only add to her sorrow.

His news when he returned was always brief and seldom varied. Reports like, "The slope is almost clear of snow." Or, "The ice is still holding fast."

There were shadows in Sam's eyes. She couldn't help noticing them, although she resisted the urge to ask him about them. What was the point when she knew he would either refuse to explain the private hell he suffered or deny its existence?

Maybe that darkness, mirroring her own bleakness, was her reason, as well, for keeping busy in the long, dull hours of the afternoon. It was either that or work herself into a state of deep despair, and she wouldn't allow herself to do that.

There was enough to keep her busy. Finding cleaning supplies in the tiny broom closet in a corner of the kitchen, she set to work sweeping and dusting, picking up and putting away everything they'd used and no longer needed.

When Sam wondered why she was bothering, Eve leaned on her broom and explained it to him. "There's enough evidence in and around the cabin for the owners to realize the place was invaded in their absence. The least I can do is to try to leave it in as neat of a condition as we found it."

He nodded, voicing no objection to her intention.

It was late afternoon when Sam returned from his last visit to the lake.

"There's a breeze picking up, a warm one from the south. The fog is beginning to shift at last."

Crossing to the fireplace, he used one of the buckets of melted snow to wet down the flames. Eve watched as what remained of the smoke drifted up the chimney.

"It will be dark soon," she observed. "That helicopter won't be buzzing around out there at night. And even if it did, they couldn't possibly see our smoke."

"I'm not going to risk it."

She thought about it for a moment before agreeing with him. Turning to the window, she gazed out at the fog. Or what was left of it. In the last light of the day, she could see the final shreds of it being driven away by a rising wind.

"We won't need a fire tonight," Sam said. "We'll be warm enough in our coats."

He went on to tell her they would sleep in the two easy chairs here in the living room, which meant returning the mattresses to the bedrooms.

"I don't want any delay in the morning," he said as she helped him haul the mattresses back to the bedrooms. "Ice or no ice, we're getting out of here as soon as it's light enough to find our way."

He was all business now. They would not share a bed on the floor tonight. Probably no bed in the future, either. Eve was all too sadly aware of that.

Nor would she be able to cook another meal for them on the kitchen stove. That, also, had her feeling a silly, sentimental regret as they disposed of the cold ashes from the fireplace, dumping them outside in a patch of snow that had yet to melt.

The sacks of food and water Eve had prepared were parked beside the front door, ready for their quick departure in the morning. The only evening meal available to them from what was left in the kitchen were the handfuls of nuts and raisins they munched on.

"I don't suppose you'll let me light one of the kerosene lamps," she said as darkness settled over the living room.

"Not a chance. I don't want any glow that could be spotted from either the ground or the air."

Although Eve thought he was being excessively cautious, she offered no objection. Maybe he was right. In any case, she was too tired to discuss it. Wrapping herself in one of the two blankets, the only bedding Sam would permit them, she curled into a corner of one of the easy chairs.

There was no reason for her not to go to sleep. Layered in her coat and the blanket, she was snug enough. But sleep didn't come. How could it when she was so aware of Sam? She couldn't see him in the darkness, but she could hear him prowling around the cabin, keeping a wakeful vigil.

His restless energy made her nervous. Made her wonder what he was thinking. But whatever those thoughts were, he kept them to himself. Nor, afraid to know them, did she ask.

Eventually, she did fall asleep. And was startled awake sometime in the middle of the night by a series of cracking noises, like the sounds of gunshots. Alarmed, she threw off her blanket and started up from the chair.

"Easy."

Sam's voice came from the direction of the window.

Turning her head, she was able to make out his form, posted there at the glass.

"It's the ice tearing apart on the lake," he calmed her. "There's moonlight out there. I can see the stuff breaking up. We've got a strong wind now moving it. With any luck, we'll have completely open water by morning."

At last!

Relieved, Eve drew the blanket over her again and went back to sleep.

The first, faint glimmer of daylight was stealing through the window when she awakened again. Stirring, she glanced at the other chair. In the end, Sam must have been overcome by fatigue. He was sprawled there, chin on his chest, long legs stretched out in front of him.

As tempting as the sight of him was, she resisted the urge to spend a few minutes admiring his totally masculine, stalwart figure. She would have to teach herself to no longer view him as anyone but the special agent who'd been charged to safely escort her to Chicago. An undertaking that would be hard for her, if not downright impossible.

Because how, Eve wondered, did you turn off powerful emotions, even if you were no longer entitled to them?

A question with no answer, which was why she turned her attention to another matter. Freeing herself from the blanket, which had somehow gotten tangled around her, she managed to get to her feet.

After folding the blanket, she draped it over her arm, intending to place it at the foot of one of the beds. She stopped first at the window to peer into the gloom.

The temperature must have dipped sharply in the hours before dawn, because a hoarfrost coated the twigs of the trees. It would glitter like a fairyland when the sun rose and then burn away rapidly into the fragrant pine air.

A pleasant observation. But not a practical one, which was why she directed her gaze to the lake below. Weak though the light still was, she was able to see that the waters were entirely free of ice. The transformation had happened with an amazing swiftness. Sam's hope to leave here by canoe had been realized.

Her gaze strayed to the sleeping figure slouched in his chair. He must have kept watch almost straight through the night to permit himself this brief, probably much-needed rest. It was still very early. She was tempted to let him sleep on for just a bit longer. But Sam wouldn't thank her for that.

As it turned out, she had no need to rouse him. A dreaded arrival took care of that.

Eve was on her way to the chair to wake him when she heard it. The sound of whirling blades, low but distinct, approaching from the north. The enemy was here! Already they were here!

Sam was instantly awake and on his feet. There must have been some clear expression of panic on her face, because he stretched out an arm, his hand closing around her wrist. Did he fear she might flee from the cabin if he didn't hold her back?

They stood there without moving, without speaking, in an attitude of frozen alertness as they listened to the now-ominous beat of the helicopter. It seemed to be heading straight for the lake, as if its pilot knew exactly where to find them.

Eve cast her gaze around the room, seeing in her mind not what was here inside the cabin but what might be outside that could betray their presence. No smoke curling from the chimney. No open shutters except for the lone window overlooking the porch, and that wouldn't be visible from the air, she remembered. Not with the roof concealing its existence. Their bootprints in the snow? She prayed not. Prayed those had all been erased in the thaw.

Were they safe?

Hard to believe when the chopper was roaring directly overhead now. When, from the sound of it, it must have swooped in low for a closer look at the cabin below. Taut seconds passed, unendurable seconds as they heard the machine circling above them. Once, twice and still again it passed above them. Then, mercifully, it swung away, the throb of it fading off into a hum.

Eve exhaled a long, quivering breath. "They're going. They didn't try to land."

Sam released her wrist. "Maybe only because there's no place for them to set down here, not with the ice on the lake gone. The only solid clearing is the slope out front, and that's too steep for any landing."

She stared at Sam, anxiety overwhelming her again. "You think they're not gone, that they know we're here?"

"They're probably considering it, anyway. Enough to want to make certain. Only they'll have to find a level clearing somewhere to put down before they can come investigating on foot. By then I plan for us to be far away from here. Come on, we're going."

Chapter 8

Sam took the lead, with both of them trotting down the hill, clutching their makeshift sacks of provisions. He paused when he reached the boatshed, looking and listening intently for any sight or sound of the helicopter. Thankfully, there was neither, making him hope that any clearing their enemy might have found was a long way off.

Tugging open the door on the landward side of the shed, he folded it back to admit light into the interior. Eve waited outside with their sacks while he made his way through the clutter to the door on the shore side, scraping it back to expose the softly lapping waters of the lake a few yards away.

Eve was inside the shed when he turned around. A shaft of light from the barely risen sun was streaming into the structure, bathing her in its golden glow. Worried though she plainly was, rumpled from her night in the chair, hair uncombed, she had never looked more enticing to him.

What in the hell are you doing?

Sucking in his breath, Sam sharply reminded himself he had no time to admire her in any condition. Whatever they had meant to each other was gone. His only duty now was to keep her safe.

"What?" she asked, puzzled by his hesitation.

"Nothing. Help me lift the canoe down from the rack, will you?"

Depositing both sacks and her shoulder bag on the floor, Eve gripped one end of the canoe and Sam the other. They removed it from the rack and loaded the two sacks into it. He dragged the canoe out of the shed and placed it on the edge of the shore, then returned for the paddle.

She must have heard him cussing under his breath. She came back inside, drawing the strap of her bag over her shoulder. "What's wrong?"

"The paddle," he said, hefting it in his hand. "The blade's cracked clear across. It'll never hold up under any pressure. There should be another one, but if there is, it's missing. I don't see it anywhere in this junk."

"Then we'll have to go back to the cabin for the other pair. We'll need both of them. It might not have occurred to you, but I do know how to paddle a canoe."

Sam gazed at her blankly. "What pair?"

"The pair mounted above the mantel. They're crossed up there like a pair of swords. The owner's idea of an appropriate decoration for a cabin, I suppose. Didn't you ever notice them?"

"I guess not." He was grateful, however, that Eve had. "Looks like we don't have a choice, but let's be quick about it."

He hated this delay. He had expected to be gone by now, not charging up the hill again. Alert for any sign of trouble, he kept searching on both sides of them. There was still no movement, no sound. He shouldn't have been bothered by the stillness, but he was. Probably a needless concern. Their situation did warrant it, though.

When they reached the cabin, he left Eve posted as a lookout on the front porch. "Wait here, and if you spot anything give a holler."

With only one narrow window unshuttered, the living room was full of shadows when he re-entered it. No wonder he'd never paid any attention to the paddles. He paid attention to them now when, leaving the front door open behind him, he approached the fireplace, swearing again softly. The blasted things were out of his reach.

Kicking a footstool into place, he climbed up on it. He expected to lift the paddles down with ease from hooks drilled into the mortar between the stones. He was mistaken. The paddles were anchored by heavy wire buried somehow into the chimney. Wire twisted around them so tightly he wasted long, precious minutes in the gloom freeing them from their mounting.

It wasn't until he backed down off the stool, a paddle in either hand, that he became aware of the total stillness. A stillness that made him suddenly uneasy.

There was no noise of any careful footstep behind him. No menacing shadow falling across the floor. It was instinct, or maybe an unclean odor he couldn't identify, that had him sensing he was no longer alone in the living room. Someone was here with him, and it wasn't Eve.

Keeping his back to the new arrival, he pretended to examine the paddles, as if making certain they weren't damaged. All the while, he tried to calculate just what his action ought to be. But there was only one option, and it wasn't a good one.

The only means of defense Sam had were the stout, wooden paddles. One of them could serve him as a weapon. The other one was a hindrance, which was why he released it. It met the floor with a clatter at the same time he flashed around in a crouch, swinging the paddle in a wide arc with all the swiftness and force of a heavy club.

He'd counted on an element of surprise, hoped to connect with his adversary and strike him down before he could act. It didn't work that way. The thug was ready for him.

Sam had only a fleeting glimpse of wire-rimmed glasses and a face like a cunning weasel before the automatic in his enemy's hand barked. The blade of the fast-moving paddle didn't stop the bullet. But it did deflect it a bit from its intended target.

Sam felt a searing pain at the outer edge of his right thigh and knew he had suffered some kind of wound. Refusing to let it stop him, he rid himself of the paddle and launched himself at the bastard before he could get off a second shot. His opponent staggered back under the impact of his attack. Sam was all over him before he could recover.

With contorted faces, grunts and curses, the two men struggled for possession of the gun. At some point, the pistol went off again. Sam figured the bullet went wild. It didn't. He felt the thug sag against him, slide down his length and topple over backward on the floor.

Breathing hard, realizing the automatic was in *his* hand now, Sam stared down at the lifeless figure sprawled at his feet. He didn't need the pool of blood bubbling up from the hole in his attacker's chest to tell him the man was dead. The sightless eyes behind the wire-rimmed glasses were clear evidence of that.

There was no mistaking the identity of the guy. He'd briefly spotted those glasses winking in the moonlight the night he had led their pursuers away from Eve. Now one of DeMarco's two boys was down. And the other henchman? Where was—?

Eve!

As fast as his injured leg could carry him, Sam sped out to the porch where his worst fear was confirmed. Gone! Eve was gone!

They must have crept up from the side of the cabin through the woods, their stealth so successful they'd managed to snatch her without a sound. Occupied with the paddles, Sam had heard absolutely nothing, not so much as the whisper of a scuffle.

Hard though it was, he made himself pause just long enough to sort it out. The one lying on the living room floor had plainly been left behind to deal with Sam while the other one must have carted off Eve. But where? Into the woods? Down to the canoe? Along the shore?

Making an effort to compose himself, he leaned out over the porch railing, scanning the area in all directions. There! The two of them were picking their way along the shoreline, Eve's captor driving her ahead of him with the muzzle of his rifle in her back.

Thank God, she was still alive! But for how long? Until he could get her back to wherever the helicopter was parked, where she would be searched and questioned at length? Or would she be flown out of here and taken to Victor DeMarco himself, who would hold her only until he got what he wanted?

Sam was wasting time on these speculations. He had to recover her before they reached that chopper. Aware of the pistol in his hand and its importance to him, he turned and limped back into the cabin. His return to the living room was necessary, much as he hated losing vital seconds.

Bending over the body, he quickly dipped his hands into several pockets until he found what he wanted. It was after he helped himself to the two spare clips for the automatic and stood erect again that, FBI special agent that he was, he was unable to prevent the realization that flashed through his mind.

The United States or Canada, it didn't matter. This was a crime scene, which sooner or later would require an investigation.

What a hell of a time to be thinking of something like this.

What he should think about, and immediately did, was the blood soaking through his pant leg, dripping on the floor. He didn't believe the bullet had lodged in his thigh. It was a flesh wound, but if he didn't curb the flow of blood he'd never manage to overtake Eve and her captor.

Freeing the scarf from around his neck, Sam bound his leg tightly above the wound. He'd probably have to loosen the tourniquet from time to time to maintain circulation. That the injury was hurting now like the devil didn't matter. He could, and would, withstand the pain.

Spare clips in a pocket of his open coat, pistol thrust into his belt, he headed swiftly back to the porch. He couldn't have been gone more than a moment or two, but Eve and her captor were already rounding the shoreline, headed along the sandy beach in the direction of the landslide stretched across the river.

Sam took off after them.

* * *

Good girl, he silently congratulated her.

Thanks to Eve, he was beginning to close the gap between them. She was making it as difficult as possible for her captor, slowing them down by stumbling over bits of driftwood and exposed rocks, pausing to recover her balance or catch her breath.

She might be buying herself time, but it wasn't because she had any knowledge that Sam was behind them. Not when he was careful to keep out of sight, hugging the edge of the woods. Ducking behind the nearest tree whenever her captor looked nervously over his shoulder, which was happening more frequently.

He must be wondering why his partner hadn't caught up to them, Sam thought. Eve must be wondering, too—that and whether Sam was dead. She had to be damn scared.

Hold on, Eve. I'm coming.

But not fast enough. The wound in his thigh was burning like hell, bleeding through the scarf to leave a trail of drops behind him. He could ignore both the pain and the seeping blood but not the need to stop periodically to loosen the tourniquet whenever his leg started to go numb on him.

It seemed to take forever for the three of them to near the landslide. Close enough now for Sam to hear a low, ominous rumble behind the barrier. The broken ice on the river, he thought.

The ice, together with the rising waters, were piling up on the other side of the dam. And the gap on the left side, now even more tightly plugged with ice chunks than before, didn't seem to be relieving the mounting pressure. Either the blocked river would spill over the top, or the force of it would tear the whole thing wide open.

And just where did that sonofabitch think he was taking Eve?

Sam watched in anger and disbelief as the butt of the rifle prodded her up the rough, uneven side of the landslide. Her captor was forcing her to the crown of the barrier, presumably intending for them to cross the ridge to the other side. The chopper had to be waiting there, out of sight behind the high, steep embankment that contained the river.

It was a risky undertaking, growing more dangerous by the second. Because the landslide was trembling like a live thing, shaken by ice and waters determined to penetrate it. And what could Sam do to stop them?

Limping seriously now, he knew his leg would never permit him to climb the ridge after them. Not when he was starting to feel light-headed from loss of blood.

Come on, McDonough, do something before you end up passing out.

They were on top of the earthen bridge now. At this distance the pistol would be no match for that rifle. But if he could use it to distract the thug long enough, it might give Eve a chance to escape.

There was an uprooted tree beside him. It would serve as an adequate cover. Flopping down on his belly behind a mass of roots, taking no chance on a bullet striking Eve, he deliberately aimed the automatic wide and fired off several shots in quick succession.

His ruse had the desired effect. The burly enemy, a bearded, mean-faced brute, whipped around, blasting the rifle repeatedly in Sam's direction. Flattening himself, he swore he could hear the bullets whistling over his head.

When he risked looking up again, he saw that Eve must have understood his action with the pistol, realized he was here behind the fallen tree. To his satisfaction, she was backing slowly away from her captor.

Knowing he had to keep the other man pinned there long enough for her to get to safety, Sam answered his fire. The landslide was bucking so violently now that, although the rifle split the air again, its aim was useless.

And then it didn't matter. Neither the rifle nor the brute struggling to steady it against his shoulder were any longer a threat. Nature, not to be resisted, decided the outcome. With a tremendous roar, driven by a savage power that had all the elements of an earthquake, the barrier collapsed.

The flood of water it released, carrying blocks of ice and debris with it, along with Victor DeMarco's henchman, swept into the lake. Sam watched the huge wave as it spread out and then leveled, absorbed by the extensive surface of the larger body of water. The river was free again, nature demonstrating its approval with a sudden, strangely peaceful calm. There was no sign of the burly thug. Hopefully, he hadn't survived.

All Sam cared about in this moment, though, was Eve. To his relief, his searching gaze found her on the other side of the river. Stranded but safe on solid ground. She was the last thing he saw before the blackness swallowed him.

He would go and regain consciousness with his pants down around his knees, Eve thought. And here she was bending over him caught in the act of…well, something that probably struck him as not entirely innocent when that was exactly what it was.

For a long moment he looked up at her in silence, that penetrating gaze of his pinned on her in wry humor.

When he finally spoke to her, his voice was like

sandpaper. "This is an interesting situation. Planning on taking advantage of me, were you?"

"That's just what I was doing. If you call dressing a bullet wound on the leg of an unconscious man taking advantage of him, that is."

His hand reached down, fingering the bandage she had taped around his bare thigh. Frowning in puzzlement, he looked from side to side, apparently realizing he was stretched out in the canoe.

"Hey, what is this? How did I—?" Before she could stop him, he'd lifted himself up far enough to recognize their location. "We're back at the boatshed. Am I dreaming?"

"Now, don't be a difficult patient. You've been enough trouble as it is." Hand against his chest, she pressed him back down against the pillows she'd squeezed under his head and shoulders. "The bleeding is stopped now, but I don't need you passing out on me again."

"And I need answers," he demanded. "Like how did I end up here? Did I go and temporarily lose my memory again?"

A pity he hadn't, Eve thought. She had liked him a whole lot better during his amnesia when he wasn't judging her. When he'd been a much kinder, more understanding Sam McDonough.

"What you lost was blood, so don't try getting up."

"You mind if I at least get my pants back up where they belong?"

"If you're careful about it."

Lifting his hips, he managed to ease his trousers up around his waist, where he secured his zipper and belt. He pushed her hand away when she started to tuck a blanket around him.

"Stop playing nurse and give me those answers. The

last thing I remember I was on one side of the river and you were on the other. What did you do? Swim across?"

She sat back on her heels, shaking her head. "There was enough of the landslide left—rocks and wedged logs sticking up from the water—that I was able to pick my way across."

"Okay, so you're back on my side, and I'm lying there like a beached whale. Then what?"

"I went for the canoe, of course. How else was I to get you back here? It was bad enough rolling and tugging you into it once I paddled out to where I'd left you."

"And the bandage?"

"There was a first aid kit up in the cabin. I brought it down, along with the paddles and the pillows."

There had also been the body of the other thug on the floor of the living room, Eve recalled, shuddering over the unpleasant image.

"Satisfied?"

"Yes. No. Are you going to make a regular practice of rescuing me, woman?"

"If I have to. And you don't need to sound so grumpy about it. What do you call taking a bullet for me?"

"My job."

It wasn't what she wanted to hear. But she knew she couldn't expect anything like the admiration he had expressed after she had pulled him out of the burning plane. That kind of tenderness had vanished when he'd recovered his memory, and it was pointless of her to go on longing for it.

He must have realized, however, that he owed her some form of gratitude. That had to be why he mumbled a softer "Maybe I was a little abrupt. I guess I should be thanking you."

"Are you? Thanking me?"

"Yeah, I am. Anything else I should know?"

"Let me see. Oh, yes, the helicopter is gone. It popped up from somewhere on the other side of the river while I was paddling the canoe over to get you back here. I watched it circle the lake. I think the pilot must have noticed the body of our other friend floating out there."

Eve had spotted that dead body herself and told Sam so. It had been another unpleasant discovery.

"I suppose," she went on, "the pilot decided he no longer had any reason to hang around. Anyway, he didn't waste time zooming out of here. The way I figure it, this third guy was never visible to us because he wasn't one of DeMarco's men, or he would have come after us, along with the other two."

Ignoring her earlier objection, Sam sat straight up in the canoe with a thunderous "And you're just now telling me this!"

"Stop getting excited. It's bad for you. We're safe enough for the moment. If that pilot was more than just hired to fly the helicopter, if he is loyal to Victor De-Marco, then it will take time for him to contact DeMarco to report what happened here."

"Which he's probably doing right now by radio. Eve, DeMarco isn't going to forget about you just because his two boys failed. Not as long as he thinks you have the evidence to send him to prison. He'll send others after you."

"I realize that. But they can't just suddenly turn up out of nowhere."

"And you can't be here waiting for them."

"What would you have had me do? Leave you there injured on the beach and head downriver on my own?"

"No, but we're not staying here. We're getting out. *Now.*"

He glanced at his watch. Then, as though not trusting it, he lifted his head to squint up at the sun. Its position in the sky would be telling him it was already past mid-morning.

"We still have most of the day left," he said. "With both of us paddling and the current with us, we ought to be able to get a long way downriver before dark. Maybe even reach a town of some kind."

"You are *not* paddling this canoe. You need to rest."

"It doesn't take a leg to paddle a canoe. I'll be fine."

"You are the most stubborn—"

"Eve, listen to me." He leaned toward her, a fierce look on his face. "I won't rest until I get you back to Chicago and under the bureau's protection. Whatever it takes. You understand me? *Whatever it takes.*"

Chapter 9

The river, which continued on its way at the other end of the lake, just as they'd surmised, presented no problems. Its current was swift enough to assist them but not so powerful that it prevented them from maintaining a steady, even course. Nor did they encounter any rapids that might have given them serious trouble.

Eve couldn't say the same for her companion.

At her insistence, Sam sat in front of her. Only this way could she keep an eye on that wounded leg of his. As it turned out, she found herself paying far more attention to other portions of his body.

The day was warm. That, along with their vigorous activity with the paddles, had them both so overheated they removed their coats. Eve couldn't take her eyes off Sam's strong back and arms. Mesmerized, she watched his muscles bunching rhythmically under his shirt as he dipped and stroked, an unconsciously erotic action that had her on edge with desire.

You're not being fair, you know. This is your fault, not his.

Not that it did her any good to go and remind herself all over again that she had been a fool to fall for him. Nor to torment herself by remembering that he hadn't forgiven her for denying him the truth about her father, even if that information had no real bearing on the case.

Oh, but the explanation for this harsher Sam Mc-Donough was much more involved than that, wasn't it? There was the darkness that on some deep level was always with him.

It was just past midday when they navigated the canoe to a still pool at the edge of the river. Both of them were ready for a rest stop, as well as hungry.

"Watch the leg," she cautioned him when he swung around on his seat to face her. She was afraid he was being much too careless with that injury.

"Stop worrying," he said, reaching for his sack of provisions. "It's coming along just fine."

Maybe he was right, she thought as they sat there drinking from their bottles of water and munching on crackers and dried fruit. Maybe she needed to worry about herself.

She couldn't seem to shake this perpetual longing for him. This wanting to have both of them naked, his hard body wrapped around hers. Not just wrapped around her but deep inside her, stroking her as he'd stroked the paddle out on the river.

It wasn't just a physical thing, either. It was as much emotional as anything else. A yearning for the tenderness he had demonstrated so freely and so often before his memory had kicked in.

Eve was convinced of it. People didn't alter their basic characters. Not overnight, anyway. If all those positive qualities, like tenderness, had surfaced during his memory loss, then they must still be there inside him, buried under the bleakness.

Did she have any right to reach for them? To make any kind of effort to save him from himself?

Why not, if you're in love with him? Shouldn't that entitle you to help him?

"Sam, can I ask you something?"

"Ask away."

"What is it that's got you all tied up in knots?"

He scowled at her. "What are you talking about?"

"You know what I'm talking about. I could see it in you from the start. You're carrying some kind of awful burden, and I don't mean getting me to Chicago. Mightn't it help to talk about it?"

His voice was brusque when he answered her. "You're imagining things. The only thing I'm suffering from is this leg."

He didn't want to discuss it. He had closed up on her, maybe even resented her for asking him about something he regarded as strictly private.

All right, she wouldn't pursue it. Not now. But she wasn't going to give up on him. Sooner or later, Eve promised herself, she was going to confront and defeat the demons that haunted him.

It was late afternoon, and Eve's arms were aching, when she heard the humming from somewhere ahead of them. She knew from the way Sam lifted his head, suddenly alert and listening intently, that he heard it, too.

"What is it?" she called to him, resting on her paddle.

"Dunno. But it isn't a helicopter."

They paddled on toward the droning noise that increased to a distinctive, steady buzzing that identified itself as some kind of machinery in operation.

Throughout their journey downriver, there had been nothing but solid forest on both sides of the stream. Now, suddenly and without warning, as they worked the canoe eagerly around a sharp bend, a huddle of buildings appeared in front of them on the right bank. The settlement that Sam had been so confident existed all along.

The small community was evidently supported by the large, gray structure that loomed at the edge of the river. It was this building that produced the constant buzzing. A sawmill.

If Eve had any doubt about that, the stacks of lumber in the yard, so freshly cut she could smell the pine and spruce, told her they had arrived at a logging operation.

"Civilization at last!" she pronounced with satisfaction.

"Or what passes for it," Sam said. "But it works."

They landed the canoe on the riverbank, dragged it up on dry land, collected their gear and headed toward the sawmill. Eve didn't like the idea of Sam putting his weight on that leg. But though he favored it, he seemed able to walk with ease.

A young man with a ponytail and a gold ring in one pierced ear leaned against the side of the building. One of the workers, Eve assumed, taking a cigarette break.

He was crushing the cigarette underfoot when he spotted them. From the expression on his face, canoers like Sam and her must be a rare sight. One that could use both bathtubs and changes of clothes.

"Where'd you two come from?"

"We're just off a wilderness canoe trip," Sam informed him.

"Not the best time of year for that."

"Yeah, we found that out, which is why we've had enough. Any chance of catching a bus or a train here?"

"Not in this place. You have to go down to Dalroy for that. There's a bus out of there that heads south twice a day."

"How do we get there?"

"Walk. And, man, you don't want to do that. Dalroy is a good twenty miles away. But, look, I live there, and if you don't mind waiting another hour until I get off work, I'll give you a lift in my pickup."

"We would appreciate that," Eve said, thanking him warmly for his offer.

"Sure. Name's Howie."

Apparently not interested in learning their names, which was just as well, Howie saluted them with a careless wave and wandered back inside the sawmill.

Prepared to wait for the guy, Eve and Sam perched themselves in the sun on a low pile of lumber. She waited until they had relieved their thirst from the bottles and finished the last of the crackers before she turned to him with her observation.

"You didn't ask him where you could find a phone." Which, since her cell phone had been destroyed by the enemy, would be their quickest method for communicating with the outside. "Why not, Sam? I would have thought contacting your squad supervisor in Chicago to let him know we're still alive and safe would be the first thing on your agenda."

He shook his head. "Bad idea."

"Because?"

"We're not safe. We're still at risk."

Eve hadn't forgotten the threat of Victor DeMarco,

their need not just to be constantly vigilant but to keep moving.

"From DeMarco, yes. Except he hasn't a clue now where to find us."

"But he could pick up our trail, if I were to inform the Chicago division where we are, ask them to help us get home."

"How?"

Sam hitched himself around to face her. "Has it ever occurred to you, Eve, that DeMarco and his people just happened to know things they weren't supposed to know? Like that Charlie Fowler was turning on him, his whereabouts and that you were joining him there? And after Fowler's death that a special agent was sent to bring you back and planned to take you by bush plane? They learned all of this and acted on it."

Eve stared at him, understanding what she should have considered long before this. "You think there's a mole in your division, someone who's been feeding DeMarco everything he needed to know. Who?"

"Haven't a clue. All I know for certain now is something I should have decided on long before this."

"Which is?"

"That I'm not trusting anyone in the bureau, even my squad supervisor. I'll get you to Chicago, but I won't hand you over for FBI protection until the informer is revealed and taken out."

"What about getting help from the Canadian authorities?"

He shook his head. "They'd insist on contacting the bureau."

"So we're on our own until we get to Chicago?"

"You mind?"

"I'll try not to complain about it."

In one regard she did mind. Feeling the way she did about him, it wasn't easy being alone with him. Not when she had to endure this perpetual longing for a man who no longer wanted her. Had there been other agents dispatched to them, or even just one more special agent, it might have eased the strain between them.

Or maybe it wouldn't. Maybe as long as he was anywhere near her, she would continue to be frustrated, whatever the company.

They were quiet for a moment. Sam went on looking at her. Whatever he was thinking, his gaze made her uneasy.

She ended their silence with an abrupt "I have another question."

"Yeah?"

"You asked Howie about a bus or a train. No mention of a plane."

"That's right. Air travel to Chicago would be a lot more convenient. It would also be a problem, what with tighter security in the airports and me with no documents. We can't afford to have any questions raised about our identities."

Relating to what he was saying and the urgency inherent in it, she nodded. "Information that could get back to the wrong people."

"Exactly."

"So we travel by bus and train."

"We do providing we can cover the fares." He eyed her shoulder bag. "How are you fixed for funds? And I don't mean credit cards."

"No, I realize that using a credit card leaves an immediate electronic trail for anyone who might be looking for it. As for cash, I have a few hundred in here." She patted the side of her bag. "Both Canadian and American dollars. And if that isn't enough…"

She hesitated.

"What?"

"There's something I haven't told you. I guess because I've been ashamed to share it."

"Let's hear it."

"It wasn't just the paddles and the first aid kit I brought away from the cabin. The dead man in the living room… Sam, I stole the money out of his wallet."

Which, considering how the mere sight of him sprawled there on the floor had been so awful, hadn't been an easy thing for her to do.

Sam stared at her for a few seconds in silence. Then, head thrown back, he whooped with laughter.

"It isn't funny."

But she enjoyed the sound of his laughter. It was the first honest mirth she had heard out of him since he had recovered his memory. It was an encouraging sign that, somewhere beneath the darkness, he was still capable of a lighter mood.

"And you feel guilty about it. Hell, Eve, it was a smart thing to do. So how much did you get? And remember, you're talking to a guy who hasn't got a red cent on him."

"I didn't stop to count it, but there's probably several hundred more."

"Which, added to what you already have, means we should make out okay."

If we're careful, she thought.

"I've got a long bed in the pickup," Howie said when he joined them. "Want me to carry your canoe with us?"

"Thanks for the offer, but we arranged for someone to collect it later on," Sam lied.

Howie told them along the way that there were no trains out of Dalroy. They would have to wait to board a train until the bus reached one of the larger towns on its route.

The young man, cheerfully refusing any payment for obliging them, dropped them off at a café that also happened to be the bus depot. Learning that the second bus of the day out of Dalroy wouldn't arrive for another hour, they settled themselves at a corner table.

The meal they ordered was the first decent food Eve had eaten since leaving the Yukon. Whatever her cooking skills, she was thankful that their dinner here involved nothing like beef jerky or powdered milk.

Sharing a seat on the bus once they boarded was another matter. Sam slept without interruption as they traveled through the night. Equally exhausted though Eve was, she found it difficult to rest with his head lolling against her shoulder.

He was much too close to her. Experiencing this physical contact, however innocent it was, was far too arousing. There was so much to be aware of—the masculine scent of him, the heat of his body against hers, the sensual shape of his bold mouth. All of it as effective as an aphrodisiac.

She was relieved when early the next morning the bus set them down in a small city along a rail line to the south. There was time before the next train to find a discount store where they bought changes of clothing for themselves, a few necessary toiletries, including a razor for Sam and a baseball cap for Eve.

"Your hair is too noticeable," he'd decided. "You need to pin it up under something, now that we'll be traveling through populated areas. I don't want you arousing any curiosity, and having someone remark about seeing you. Word has a way of traveling."

He was being overly cautious again, but after having been snatched by the enemy back at the cabin, Eve understood his concern. They cleaned up and changed in the restrooms at the train depot, where Sam shaved off his whiskers.

They looked far less like two people who had just emerged from the wilderness when they boarded the train. In fact, Eve was convinced they could have been any ordinary couple. They certainly elicited no special interest from any of the other passengers, unless you counted the women who couldn't help eyeing Sam in his snug new jeans. And that, given his blatant sexiness, was certainly understandable.

Sam, however, continued to exercise alertness. Not that their long journey toward the border ever posed any risk. Except to her heart.

Pleasant enough to her, never anything but concerned about her welfare, Sam gave her no reason to complain. If only…

If only what, Eve? If only there wasn't this barrier he's so careful to maintain between the two of you? He on one side, you on the other.

But that's just the way it was now, and he wouldn't let her penetrate that wall, no matter how hard she tried. Not emotionally.

Although it might just be her imagination, she sensed sometimes that he still desired her. But if that were true, he never expressed it by either word or action, preferring his own dark thoughts over her company.

Aching for him, equally alone with her sore heart,

Eve couldn't wait to have this whole journey behind her, including whatever happened in Chicago, so she could make some effort to put her despair behind her.

Chapter 10

Sam had managed to pick up a travel guide at one of their train stops.

"What did you learn?" Eve questioned him after he spent a silent half hour consulting it as they rolled through the grasslands of Saskatchewan, where the snow was gone without a trace.

"Our destination for crossing the border."

"Which is?"

"I'll let you know when we get there."

He watched those expressive eyebrows of hers, which seldom failed to register her moods, lift with a mix of puzzlement and irritation. "Why do you always have to make a mystery of everything?"

"Because I like to be sure before I commit myself."

Those eyebrows drew together with impatience. He could see that impatience warring with her stubborn pride. Pride must have won the contest, because she ended up turning her head away in silence.

That was on the day coach of the train hours ago. They were no longer seated on the train now but at the table of a Nordic-themed café in the sizable town of Calhoun along the Canadian-U.S. border. The table where they were drinking coffee was located beside a front window overlooking the ports of exit and entry a few hundred feet away.

Eve was no longer able to maintain her silence on the subject. "All right, so why did you choose Calhoun for us to leave the train?"

"You notice all the shops in town?"

"How could I help not noticing them when you had me walking up and down the streets checking them out?"

"Lots of bargains in them, weren't there? Some of it the kind of merchandise Americans can't get across the border, and plenty of traffic in those shops buying it. Just as the guide said."

"And that matters how?"

"*Day* traffic, Eve. They drive over from the Montana side in the morning, and by late afternoon they cross back."

Eve cast her gaze in the direction of the two border ports, where both the Canadian and American officers were anything but busy at their stations. But before much longer…

Sam could see her eyebrows now expressing understanding.

"The officers at the American gate will soon have all they can do processing the traffic back through to the Montana side," she said.

"So occupied," he added, "they won't have time to waste on anyone who doesn't look either suspicious or have the right documents."

That, anyway, was what Sam was hoping for.

Eve went on looking at the American gate. Then, suddenly and in alarm, her gaze cut back to him. "Sam," she remembered, "you don't have those documents. Your passport and FBI credentials were destroyed in the plane."

"No, but you do have the proper identification to go through the gate."

"What are you telling me? That you mean to send me on to Chicago on my own?"

"I'd never do that—not unless it turns out there's no other way."

"Then how—" She caught herself with realization. "You're going to sneak across the border. That's what you intend to do, isn't it?"

"If I can manage it, and if I wait until dark I should be able to slip across."

They were already talking in low tones, even though no other table near them was occupied. But Eve dropped her voice to an urgent whisper as she leaned toward him across the table.

"Sam, that's dangerous. There could be electric fences and border patrols. You'll be caught."

It wasn't a moment for amusement, but he couldn't prevent a smile. "Eve, the Canadian-U.S. border is thousands of miles long. How do you imagine it could ever be fenced, especially in sparsely populated, rough terrain like this? As for patrols, there aren't enough of them to go around, except in sensitive areas."

"Even so, it's risky. Especially with that leg of yours."

"Will you stop worrying about the leg? It's not a problem." But there was one that did concern him. "You're the one who's at risk."

"What are you thinking now?"

"That the bureau has to be wondering whether we're

still alive and, if so, where we are. They could have issued a general bulletin to be on the watch for us, and if your name should turn up on a list at that gate…"

"They'll be too busy to consult it. Isn't that what we're counting on? That I won't be stopped and held?"

"I'm hoping that's the case. Look, Eve, I wouldn't ask you to do this, if there was any other way."

"There is. I can go with you, sneak across the border with you."

He shook his head emphatically. "Absolutely not. If I should by any chance run into a border patrol, they'll be armed. And if they're not trained professionals, they could end up shooting first and asking questions afterwards. No, you'll be much safer at the gate out there."

"I don't like any of this, Sam."

"I don't, either, but that's the way it has to be," he insisted. He looked around. "We're going to start attracting attention if we go on sitting here. I think we'd better blend in by going back to those shops. Besides, we need to make you look as innocent as possible when all the American day-trippers crowd in here, like you're one of them. That means carrying some packages. Come on," he said, rising from the table, "let's pay our bill and go shopping for a few bargains."

Sam had regretted her reluctance when they'd left the café. He felt even more sorry for her when she had to pass up a set of expensive kitchen knives in one of the shops.

"What I wouldn't give for these," she said, admiring the set longingly. "They're just what I've been looking for and can't find in St. Louis. Don't say it. I know. I can't afford to spend the money on them."

They ended up buying several cheap souvenirs for her. By the time they returned to the ports, it was late afternoon and cars were lined up at the Canadian exit gate, each waiting their turn to go back over the border.

"I didn't think about this," Sam muttered. "They're all in cars, and you're on foot. That could make you a noticeable exception."

It was Eve who devised an acceptable story for herself.

"If they ask, I'll tell them I didn't want to bother with a car I wouldn't need. That a friend dropped me off on the U.S. side and is picking me up when I come back through."

Sam considered her plan. It was simple but sound. "Good enough." He hesitated before going on with a solemn "Eve, there's something else. If I shouldn't make it across—"

"But you will! You have to!"

"But if I shouldn't, you'll have to go on to Chicago by yourself." He gave her some essential instructions. "Don't try to travel straight through. Keep switching from trains to buses to confuse anyone who might be on your trail. When you reach Chicago, head directly to this lawyer your father told you about. If Fowler hadn't trusted him completely, he would never have mentioned him to you. You know his name?"

She nodded. "Alan Peterman. Charlie had me memorize both that and his address."

"Good, because I'm relying on him to help you. No contact with anyone else until he makes certain it's safe for you to turn yourself in for secure protection."

"Sam, none of this is necessary. All I need to know is where we're going to meet."

He had thought earlier about trying to locate a public phone, maybe even buying a prepaid one, in order to find a room somewhere where they could safely rendezvous. But this action would have involved his making inquiries, maybe a number of them, some of which were certain to be remembered. Not to mention the possibility of leaving the kind of trail he didn't want to chance. He'd rejected the idea without even mentioning it to Eve.

His gaze strayed now to the scene across the border. He was thoughtful for a moment. She was waiting with an expression of expectancy when he turned his attention back to her, dangling the sunglasses in her hand by one of its stems.

"It looks like Elbow Bend on the other side is almost as big as Calhoun. I'm sure there are motels over there. Find an inexpensive one, out on the edge of town if you can. Get a single room and wait for me there."

"How on earth are you going to know which motel and which room?"

He looked at the baseball cap under which her rich, russet-colored hair was tucked. "When it gets dark, tie your cap to the doorknob outside your room. It may take me a while to search for the right motel and the right door, but I'll find you."

Find her? Hell, if he failed to make it across the border, this might be the last time he would see her. The thought of parting from her here, of sending her off on her own, tugged at his gut.

He hated the idea of watching her walk away from him. As if it might be the last time they would part from each other, he stood there imprinting her image on his mind. Her lush mouth, creamy complexion, luminous green eyes, the shallow cleft in her chin.

He could bear looking at those. But not that sensational body. Not when over these last few days he'd fought himself to keep his hands off her. To do otherwise would have been fatal.

All he could manage was to remind himself how relieved

he would be when this whole thing was done with. When he could safely hand her over and walk away. Eve didn't need someone like him, all messed up inside, complicating her life. She was too fine of a woman for that.

"One more thing," he said, his voice dangerously husky, threatening to expose the emotions churning inside him. "Keep the drapes closed and your door locked. Don't open it to anyone but me."

"Understood. How long do you think you'll be getting to me?"

"Impossible to say when I don't know what delays I might encounter. Probably a couple of hours after nightfall at least. You'd better go now."

She gazed at him for a long moment with those wide eyes that had him struggling with the urge to kiss her goodbye. Only when she slid the sunglasses over her nose, shading her eyes from his view, was Sam able to restrain himself.

In silence, without another word, Eve turned and walked away from him. He went on standing there, needing to make certain that she passed through the American gate.

With an endless tension gripping his whole body, he watched her move slowly forward in the line. There was no delay at the Canadian station. The guards there didn't care about who was leaving, only those wanting to enter. She was passed on down to the U.S. gate.

Sam held his breath as Eve removed her passport from her bag, displayed it to the young American guard who briefly examined it, poked through the contents of her shopping bag, exchanged what appeared to be no more than a few casual words with her, then waved her on through.

She had crossed the border without a challenge. Sam was able to breathe again.

He lingered there for another minute until she mingled with the traffic on the other side and disappeared from view. Only then did he walk away, intending to find a place where he could wait for darkness, when he would make his way out into the countryside. And back to Eve.

Sam, Sam, where are you?

It was after eleven o'clock, and Eve was frantic, hating the sight of the cramped room, feeling trapped within its walls.

How many Starlight Motels could there be across the country? she'd wondered. Maybe most of them were like this one, with outdated furniture, worn carpets and nothing to distinguish them from all the other Starlight Motels, except for the cheap prints on the walls. This one featured garish scenes of the Rocky Mountains.

Eve had grown so sick of looking at those pictures she had gone into the adjoining bathroom and sat on the toilet seat. But this was no better. It made no difference where she settled. Here or in the bedroom, her worry about Sam was just as deep and constant.

In the beginning, even more than two hours after nightfall, she had made every effort to exercise patience. Told herself there could be any number of understandable factors delaying Sam's arrival.

It might have been necessary for Sam to travel a considerable distance away from Calhoun before he was able to find some spot isolated enough to ensure a safe crossing. That achieved, he would have faced a long hike back in the dark and then the need to find the motel with her cap on the door. All of it requiring time.

But this much time?

In the end, her patience had morphed into scenarios that had no harmless explanations. He had lost his way. The injured leg had failed him or, worse, had been torn open while he'd crawled through a tangle of barbed wire. He'd been discovered sneaking across the border and was now in a jail cell.

All those fears had been real to her. And any one of them carried the same outcome. Sam was not going to arrive. He was never coming, and tomorrow morning she would be alone when she boarded the first bus out of Elbow Bend.

Eve was sick with dread, prepared to unlock the door and check the knob again to be sure the cap was still there and hadn't somehow been removed, even to risk venturing outside to hunt for him, when a sharp rap sounded on the door.

Breathless with a sweet relief, she flew to the door, where she heard Sam on the other side calling out a low "It's me, Eve."

Fumbling with the lock, she opened the door and swung it back. He scarcely had time to slip inside and lock the door behind him before she recklessly launched herself into his arms. The sight of him was so wonderful she didn't care what the consequences might be. She wanted him holding her, his body pressed tightly against hers.

The miracle of it was he seemed to need the same long-denied embrace. More than that, better than that, he bent his head to cover her face with a series of feverish kisses.

Kisses she welcomed with equal abandon, and between which she managed wild murmurs of "I thought you weren't coming. I thought maybe a border patrol stopped you. That they'd have dogs with them—vicious dogs."

He chuckled, responded with an easy "No patrols, no dogs. The only thing I risked out there was the possibility of hidden sensors. Seems like, if they were there, I must have avoided them."

There was no talk after that. There were just his kisses that branded her cheeks and throat, nipped the lobes of her ears. Kisses that escalated, with his mouth finally claiming her own.

Eve could hear her moans as his tongue parted her lips, seeking and achieving the entry she'd wanted for far too long.

It was a sizzling connection, a man and a woman communicating their desire for each other on the deepest, most intimate level. A mutual exploration that involved not just the contact of their moist lips and tongues, but flavor, scent and, for Eve at least, emotions that spiraled out of control.

Maybe it was that way for Sam, too. Maybe this was what the groans low in his throat expressed, a release of the restraint he'd exercised so rigidly ever since the recovery of his memory.

Whatever the explanation, when he lifted his mouth from hers, he registered his urgency with a raw "It just about killed me seeing you walk away to that gate."

"How do you think I felt leaving you there?"

"We can do something about that separation."

For this one night, anyway.

Sam didn't add those words. But, spoken or unspoken, she sensed them. She refused to let them matter. Whatever tomorrow, or all the tomorrows after that, might bring, she was willing to settle for tonight.

Demonstrating his own eager readiness for this, his

arms still around her, Sam backed her up to the queen-sized bed. All it needed was a nudge from him to send her falling onto the bed.

Did he release her? He must have, but with her every nerve ending on fire she couldn't be sure. If he had, he joined her instantly, his strong body covering hers, pinning her to the bed.

His hands were all over her, stroking her breasts, sliding over her hips, parting her thighs. Eve felt the heat of one of those hands squeezed up hard against the juncture of her legs, his long fingers rubbing that most sensitive area of her body so skillfully it didn't seem to matter that she was still fully dressed.

It mattered to Sam. "The hell with this," he growled. "I want us naked. I want every part of me feeling every part of you with nothing in the way."

Lifting himself away from her, he began to tear at his clothes in a frenzy. Garments flew off the bed in every direction. She watched in dry-mouthed fascination as his body swiftly emerged. The sleek muscles of his arms and chest, his narrow hips and long legs And between them the dark-framed shaft that defined his manhood.

"You, too, Eve," he commanded her.

With trembling fingers, she obeyed him, shedding her clothes and casting them aside. Somehow in their mad scramble, he managed to remove the coverlet from beneath them, exposing the sheets to the same naked state as their bodies.

Eve's emotions were in a turmoil of sensation when he pressed her down against those sheets. The joy of his hard flesh against her soft flesh. His hands licking down her sides, tracing the contours of her body. His deep voice demanding, "What do you want, Eve? Tell me what you want."

"You, Sam. Just you."

"Like this?"

She gasped when, head dipping, his mouth closed on the nipple of one of her breasts, suckling so strongly that she cried out in blind pleasure.

"Or maybe this?" he asked, moving on to her other breast, where his tongue tugged the peak into a diamond-hard rigidity.

"Enough," she pleaded.

"No, not nearly enough."

And it wasn't. She knew it wasn't, even though she was fast losing all control. Did lose it when his mouth descended to the mound between her thighs, found and fastened on the nub within the center of that mound. Refused to release it until Eve was bucking in a wet, furious climax.

Had the spasms been long enough for Sam to extract a condom from the supply in his coat pocket, sheathe himself with it? Again without her awareness? He had to have done so because, when the last waves subsided, he was poised above her and ready.

Just before he joined himself to her, he captured her gaze. Eve found herself looking directly into those compelling, brown eyes. The amber lights in them had never been brighter. Or affected her more deeply, conveying— What? She was afraid to call it anything like love, settling instead for a profound tenderness. That she knew he was capable of.

For now it had to be enough.

With his gaze still holding hers, Sam's swollen length surged into her. He barely gave her time to adjust to him before he began to deliver a series of long, deep strokes. Slow at first, then increasing in tempo.

She dug her fingers into his solid back, clutching at

him, endeavoring to match his rhythms with her own in a storm of lovemaking unlike any they had engaged in before.

How was it possible, Eve wondered, that a drab, ordinary motel room could be transformed by their passion into something that was pure magic? But magic it was as Sam's body consumed hers, lifting her into a second release so intense it had her crying out his name.

His own satisfaction followed almost immediately. Sealing their completion with a gentle kiss, he rolled away from her, gathering her close against his side.

For long moments, she savored the mellow aftermath of their union. It should have been all she needed. It wasn't. Not when, God help her, her love for him was so hungry it called out for a commitment.

That, Eve knew, was not possible. Not as long as Sam continued to keep his dark, bitter secret locked inside himself. Maybe not even if he released it to her. But she could no longer tolerate his emotional withdrawal. Felt she had a right to share his pain, to understand it.

Fortifying herself with a deep breath of air, she lifted herself on one elbow to look down on him. "Sam?"

"Mmm?"

"There's something I have to ask you."

"Yes?"

She felt him stir uneasily against her side, as if anticipating something unpleasant. Which, for him, it probably would be.

"I think you know what it is. Knew back on the river I wasn't going to let it rest. I want to know what you've been hiding from me. What's got you suffering so terribly inside."

He shot up to a sitting position on the bed, shoving his

hand through his hair. "I told you then, and I'm telling you now—"

"I know what you told me, that you're not suffering from anything. I didn't believe it on the river, and I don't believe it now. Why won't you let me help you?"

Chapter 11

He was angry. She could see it in the way he scowled down at her, hear it in his voice.

"Why the hell can't you just let it go?"

Eve wasn't going to permit his resentment to stop her—not this time. She sat up beside him and put her hand on his arm, expecting him to shake it off. He didn't. That much was in her favor.

"Because I care," she answered him softly. "Probably far too much, but there it is."

He was silent. Maybe that, too, was a good sign.

"Sam, we both know you're hurting. Why can't you trust me?"

He laughed. A brittle laugh. "Yeah, I know. You want to help me. And just how do you figure on doing that when the best shrink in the Chicago division couldn't manage it over the past ten months?"

"At least you admit you have a problem. That's something, anyway."

"Uh-huh, I have a problem. And it's going to stay *my* problem."

It was time, she decided, to take off the velvet gloves. To challenge him on the kind of tough level he would understand and relate to. She hoped.

"You're afraid," she accused him. "That's it, isn't it? You're afraid to let me know that Special Agent McDonough, who can deal with the worst of the bad boys and win, is actually capable of being vulnerable."

"Why you little—"

His expression was so thunderous that for a moment Eve thought he was going to grip her by the shoulders and shake her until she pleaded for his forgiveness. But that wasn't Sam's way.

Regaining a measure of self-control, he confronted her with a resigned, weary "All right. You want to hear it, then hear it. Her name was Lily."

Was. The past tense. Meaning that, whoever Lily was or had been, she was gone. Eve could guess from the finality in his tone what that meant. Lily was dead. How and why that mattered so deeply to Sam, she had yet to learn.

"Just like the flower," he went on. "All fragrant and fragile. On the outside, that is. On the inside Lily was strong. Fresh out of Quantico and determined to succeed."

"An FBI agent."

"One they paired with me when she arrived from the academy. It's typical for new agents to be assigned to senior, experienced agents. The best method for learning in the field."

"And she became more than just a partner to you, didn't she, Sam?"

Why else would he be feeling Lily's loss with such awful pain?

"It was the worst kind of mistake two agents can make, but, yeah, we ended up having an affair."

"Did you fall in love with her, Sam?"

His broad shoulders elevated in a little shrug. "I don't know. I suppose that's what it was."

Eve had no right to feel the stab of jealousy she experienced, not when the poor woman was dead. Loving Sam as she did herself was no excuse. She still disliked herself for that jealousy, tried to get past it with a quick "What happened?"

"I made a serious mistake. We'd gotten information about an art heist going down in a Chicago gallery. This gang had been operating for months throughout the Midwest, hitting other galleries, as well as collections in private homes."

Which, if the thefts had been that widespread, crossing state lines, would be a matter for the FBI, Eve presumed.

"I was in charge of the team that went in there that night," Sam continued. "Understand, we're careful about what assignments we permit the rookies to be any part of. Nothing dangerous until they're more seasoned. But art theft…well, it almost never includes violence, not like drug busts."

He paused for a few seconds while Eve waited silently, wondering if he would refuse to go on. When he did make the effort to relate the rest, his voice quickened, biting out the words.

"Lily was eager to be included in the action. Begged me not to leave her out. I didn't see the risk in it. Didn't let myself consider the possibility that these weren't like the usual art thieves. Guys who played it safe. Surrendered without endangering themselves. Seldom armed, and if they are, unwilling to use their weapons."

Sam shoved his face down into hers, his eyes blazing.

"Do you see, Eve? Lily was green. She wasn't to blame for being careless and letting herself get caught in the cross fire. I was responsible. I should have known better. Should have protected her. Whatever Internal Affairs decided afterwards, I was to blame for all of it."

"Sam, you can't punish your—"

"Don't say it! I screwed up! That's why Lily died! And that was only half the hell! You wanna know the whole of it, Eve?"

As stricken as his face was now with grief and guilt, she wasn't sure that she did. In any case, he didn't wait for her choice.

"She was pregnant with my kid when she died. I didn't know. She didn't tell anyone in the division. Afraid, I suppose, that if anyone knew before she showed, she wouldn't be allowed in the field. Would be tied to a desk."

"When did you—"

"At her funeral. Her mother told me. That I'd not only killed her daughter, I'd killed my own baby."

"Oh, Sam, you didn't deserve that!"

"Yeah, I did. She knew what all the others wouldn't see. That it was my fault. And what did I do about it? Nothing but go out that night and get myself stinking drunk, as if that would help." He glanced down with a twisted smile at his arm, around which the tattoo of the dragon was wrapped. "That's how I ended up with this, although I don't have any memory of it. A fitting souvenir, huh, something to remind me for the rest of my days what a bastard I was."

The smile was gone when he looked up at her again, his voice wooden, without expression.

"That's all of it, Eve. You've heard everything. Are you satisfied now?"

The anguish on his face tore her up inside. She longed to put her arms around him, to hold him close, but she knew he wouldn't welcome her comfort.

"There are no answers, Eve," he said flatly. "Haven't been in all the months I was on leave from the division. But thanks for trying."

He sank down again at her side, silent, staring up vacantly at the ceiling. The room that had been filled with such magic earlier now felt nothing but dreary to her.

She had been prepared to fight for him, to save him from himself. But she had lost the battle. His pain remained. So deeply, tightly rooted that it crippled him emotionally.

Eve didn't know what else she could try to help him. Nor would he appreciate any further effort from her. Didn't he already resent her for forcing him to surrender his story to her?

She had no better example of that than when she woke up in the middle of the night to find Sam no longer beside her. When she lifted her head from the pillow in search of him, the dim glow of the night-light from the bathroom showed her that he had moved over to the shabby sofa.

If this was what it meant to be devastated, then that was exactly what she was.

This was the first hot shower he'd had since leaving Chicago, and Sam should have been silently expressing his gratitude for it. Which he would have been doing, had there been room for anything other than the emotions chewing him up inside.

Much as he hated to acknowledge it, he'd gone and

fallen in love with Eve Warren. What a damn fool thing for him to do.

He had to resist it, of course. Whatever happened after this morning, he had to resist it. Fight to cure himself of that love. He couldn't deal with it. Not after Lily.

And he refused to let Eve know about this struggle. Bad enough that he had told her all about Lily, leaving himself not just vulnerable, but exposed and raw. Not the kind of man he wanted to be for any woman, least of all Eve.

He turned under the hot spray, rinsing the shampoo off his hair while telling himself that, after committing the error last night of making love to Eve, it should be a cold shower.

What in the name of God had possessed him to become intimate with her like that again? There had been an excuse for the passion they had shared during his memory loss. But not last night. Not when he should have known how disastrous the consequences could be if he let his desire rule him.

And his desire had ruled him. Eve had just been far too tempting to resist.

But never again, he promised himself, soaping his body vigorously. No more failures on that score. Because Eve didn't deserve a head case like him. She was worth far more than that.

So, McDonough, he ordered himself, *you don't trust yourself to do anything from now on but protect her, as you should have protected Lily.*

As far as sex was concerned, Sam knew he had a healthy appetite. Knew he wasn't capable of any prolonged celibacy. When he wanted sex again, and sooner or later he would, he'd hunt for it where he'd found it in those bleak months after Lily's death. With women who wanted nothing more complicated than one-night encounters.

No more emotional involvements that could hurt, as he must be hurting Eve. As he, himself, was hurting.

When this assignment was over and done with, when Eve was safe from all harm, he would let her go. Tough though it would be, he would somehow manage to walk away from her. But until then...

Alternating between trains and buses as they did, the journey to Chicago was a long, slow one. And for Eve a difficult one.

Though physically Sam remained close at her side almost every minute, constantly vigilant, emotionally he was detached. He never thawed since that night in the motel. The barrier had not only gone up between them again, it was more solid than ever, leaving Eve distraught and not knowing what she could do about it.

Would this trip never end?

"I don't see why we have to keep covering our tracks like this," she complained. "If Victor DeMarco's people are out there hunting for us, there's been no sign of them. And with you refusing to contact your division, there's no way this mole you're convinced exists can feed them any information. They haven't a clue where we are."

"It pays to be careful," was his stubborn response.

So careful, she knew, that he continued to carry the pistol he'd taken from the thug back at the cabin, loaded and ready for any emergency. Sam was taking no risk.

Spring was not only fully under way when they arrived by train at Union Station in Chicago, it was so warm it felt like summer.

"We certainly don't need these winter coats," Eve said

as they walked side by side along the platform after descending from the train.

"No," Sam agreed. "In fact, we could be drawing attention to ourselves even carrying them."

"We could stow them in a locker here in the station," she suggested.

"Yeah, except where do I conceal the gun?" He eyed her shoulder bag. "You got room in there for it?"

"I can squeeze it in."

"All right, but stick close so I can grab it if I need it."

They waited until they were alone in one of the locker aisles to make the switch. After securing the coats in a locker, they headed for the nearest exit.

Sam's sharp eyes missed nothing on their way to the street. It was highly unlikely that any of DeMarco's people would be here watching the station. But Sam, she knew, was not going to let his guard down for a single moment.

Eve, herself, was conscious only of him. Had he been planning on delivering her immediately to his squad supervisor, this might have been her last opportunity to gaze at him. Not that she needed to make any effort to imprint on her memory the image of the tall, rangy figure striding beside her. That chiseled face, with its bold, sensual mouth and brooding eyes would be with her forever.

Still, if this should turn out to be her final few hours with him, she would count them as precious. Something to treasure when she was back in St. Louis. Or maybe to wish she could forget when it became vital for her to try to get over him. As sooner or later she would be wise to do.

The sun was blinding when they emerged on the sidewalk. A line of taxis waited at the curb for fares from incoming trains. Eve expected Sam to usher her immediately into one of those cabs and was surprised when he drew her back into the shade cast by the building, where they talked in low tones, although no one was paying any attention to them.

"Why this delay?" she wondered. "I thought you'd be anxious to get me somewhere safe as soon as possible."

"Have you forgotten I'm not taking you anywhere near the bureau until that mole has been taken down?"

"I haven't forgotten. Then where *are* we going?" He was being mysterious again, having failed to share his intention with her in advance. It wouldn't do her any good to be irritated with him about it. That's just the way Sam was.

"To Fowler's lawyer for starters," he said.

"I know that was your plan for me when there was the possibility you wouldn't make it across the border, that I'd have to go on alone. But now with—"

"Look, Eve, I need a bargaining chip, something to convince Frank Kowsloski" —who was Sam's squad supervisor, she knew— "that there is a mole, and he's got to set the machinery in motion to root him out."

"I don't know your squad supervisor, but I can't imagine he's going to like your blackmailing him like that."

"He won't, but that's just too bad, because I won't hand you over to him until he agrees to play ball."

She knew it would be pointless to argue with him about it. "And you think the lawyer might be able to provide us with this bargaining chip. Like what?"

"Ideally, a copy of DeMarco's fraudulent tax records."

"That you'll withhold until the mole is out of the way. What makes you think Charlie gave that copy to Alan Peterman?"

"It has to be somewhere, and since he didn't leave it

with you, why not the lawyer he not only trusted but who was his close friend? Come on, we're wasting time. Let's grab one of these cabs."

They didn't talk as the taxi carried them through the Loop, then turned north on Michigan Avenue. Feeling it was safer now not to look at Sam, she concentrated her attention on the view through the window on her side.

She found the big-city traffic and crowded sidewalks, both in downtown Chicago and here on the Magnificent Mile, just a bit overwhelming after the time they'd spent in the Canadian wilderness. What she did enjoy, however, was the sight of the huge tubs located at intervals along the sidewalks, each of them blazing with tulips in every hue.

The lawyer's residence was located on a quiet, tree-lined street just off the Gold Coast. As Eve had explained to Sam after giving their driver the address, "Charlie told me Alan Peterman is semiretired and practices out of his house now. He only sees his regular clients."

The address they were delivered to was a handsome, two-story brick row house from an earlier era. Eve paid the fare from the dwindling funds in her bag. She didn't mention her concern about that to Sam. She could only suppose, now that he was back in Chicago, he would have ready access to his own money.

Climbing the steps to the front door, with Sam directly behind her, she rang the bell. The door was answered a moment later by an elderly, stoop-shouldered man with scant, gray hair and a benign face. He wore a soiled apron tied around his waist and carried a long-handled wooden spoon as though it were a baton.

Servant or lawyer? Eve wasn't sure. "We're looking for Mr. Peterman."

"You're speaking to him."

"Mr. Peterman, I'm—"

"I know who you are. Charlie had a photo of you in his condo. I've been expecting you. Come in."

The lawyer gazed at Sam with a direct curiosity after he had closed the door behind them. Eve quickly introduced him. "This is Sam McDonough."

She wasn't certain whether Sam would want her to add an explanation to his name, but he took care of that when he shook Alan Peterman's free hand.

"I'm the FBI special agent who escorted Eve back here from the Yukon."

The lawyer didn't seem surprised by Sam's identity. How much did he know? Eve wondered.

"Let's go back to my office," he said, leading the way down a broad corridor.

Eve's brief impression of the house was of an understated elegance, where comfort took precedence over formality. She was more interested in the delectable odor in the air, something that included onions. They had clearly interrupted the lawyer as he was preparing something in the kitchen.

He verified that when they arrived at the door of his office. "Go on in and make yourselves at home. I'll just be a minute. I've got spaghetti sauce on the stove that needs stirring."

Eve found herself seconds later seated in a leather-covered chair with Sam next to her in a matching one. Both chairs faced a massive mahogany desk behind which were floor-to-ceiling shelves filled with books. Legal volumes, she supposed.

"I think he must already know Charlie Fowler is dead," Sam said.

Before they could speculate about what else Alan Peterman might know, he returned. He had rid himself of both the apron and the spoon.

"I turned the heat low under the sauce and left it simmering," he said, settling himself in an office chair behind the desk. "It's always better when it cooks a long time. But you'd know all about that."

Her father must have told his friend about her culinary ambitions. Maybe a great deal more than that.

The lawyer switched his attention from Eve to Sam. "The FBI has already been here to interview me. They told me Charlie is dead. No details, of course, and I didn't ask for them. I'm assuming it wasn't the cancer." His gaze went back to Eve. "We both have a reason to grieve."

Sam hunched forward in his chair. "The FBI. Did you hand anything over to them?"

His expression sober now, the lawyer glanced at Sam. He has to be thinking, Eve thought, that, as an FBI agent, Sam should already know the answer to this. But the lawyer didn't pursue it.

"Yes," he said. "A copy of this." Opening a drawer, he produced a document that he placed in front of them on the blotter. "It's Charlie's will. This is another copy you can take with you. The original is in my safe. I think you know its contents, Eve, since he was planning to tell you."

"Yes, he did."

"Then you understand that his entire estate goes to you. The will will have to go through probate before you can collect anything. I'll handle that for you."

Eve saw no reason to tell him she had no intention of touching the money, that she planned to donate all of it to cancer research.

"There's also this," he said, extracting a key from the

same drawer and sliding it toward her across the desk.
The key had a tag attached to it. Eve could see an address
printed on the tag. "It's a spare key to Charlie's condo.
The condo and all its contents are part of the estate, so
they belong to you now. As long as you don't take away
any of those contents until the will is settled, there's no
reason you can't visit the place. I understand the FBI is
finished with it."

Yes, Eve realized, they would have searched the
condo. And DeMarco's people, too, had probably found
a way to get in there, all of them hunting for those tax
records.

She and Sam also wanted the elusive copy of the records. Maybe it didn't exist, although Charlie had promised the FBI he would hand it over when he returned from
the Yukon. But so far their meeting with Alan Peterman
had not gained them any knowledge of the records. She
glanced at Sam, wondering if he was disappointed in the
outcome of their visit. If so, there was no evidence of this
on his face.

"I'll be in touch when the will has been cleared," the
lawyer said, indicating an end to the meeting. "Do you
have a phone number where I can reach you?"

"Uh, not yet."

"Why don't you call me when you do?" Removing a
business card from another drawer, he got to his feet and
came around the desk to hand it to her.

Eve accepted the card, tucking it into her bag along
with the key and the will. She and Sam stood, prepared
to be conducted out of the office.

"I assume there's nothing else then?" Eve said, making
a last effort before they thanked the lawyer and left.

"That's it for now, but as I said—" He stopped, holding
up a hand. "Ah, I almost forgot. There is something else."

He chuckled softly. "At my age, the memory isn't always as sharp as you'd like it to be. But still good enough, I hope, to recall where I..."

Eve watched the lawyer cross the room to a file cabinet, afraid to believe this was anything important.

"Yep, I was right. Here it is," Peterman said, scooping a plastic bag with whatever it contained out of one of the drawers. "Charlie made me promise to give this to you if you came to see me."

He returned with the bag and placed it in Eve's hand. From the shape and weight of it, she realized it was a book. When she looked inside the bag, she saw that it was a children's book. The jacket was so fresh it had to have been newly purchased. What on earth—?

Her eyebrows must be registering puzzlement, Eve thought, because the lawyer shrugged. "Charlie's gifts, bless his heart, didn't always make sense. I know I got some odd ones from him every Christmas. Well, if we're finished..."

Chapter 12

They stood on the sidewalk outside Alan Peterman's house, Eve clutching the plastic bag.

"You don't think..."

"We won't know until we examine it," Sam said.

She started to open the bag.

"Not here," he said, his hand covering her own.

She wished he wouldn't touch her like that. Innocuous though he meant it, any physical contact from him stirred longings in her that couldn't be satisfied. Maybe he understood this and that's why he immediately withdrew his hand.

"Look," he said, gazing up the street in the direction of Lake Michigan, "Lincoln Park is just a block over. Let's go there and find someplace private."

He was still being careful, she realized. That's why he kept a sharp lookout as they headed toward the park.

They found a bench screened by tall lilacs that would

soon come into flower. At present, though, the lilacs meant nothing more than a safe spot where they could not be easily observed.

"All right," Sam said when they were seated on the bench. "Let's see what that book has to offer."

Eve had already identified the volume as an anthology of favorite fairy tales when she peeked inside the bag back in the lawyer's office. Now Sam could see that for himself when she removed the book from the bag.

"This have any meaning for you?" he asked her.

"I haven't a clue."

"Is there anything else inside the bag?"

"Nothing. Not even a store receipt."

"Then whatever he wanted you to know must be inside the book."

Eve upended the book by its spine and shook it vigorously. Had there been something like a letter or a note tucked between the pages, it would have dropped into her lap. There was no evidence of either.

"Maybe he wrote something directly on one of the pages."

The book flat on her lap now, she began to turn the pages over one by one with Sam looking on closely. They discovered no message scrawled on any of those pages. Nor had any passages that might have conveyed a meaning been underlined.

"Sam, this is useless," she said when they reached the last page. "There's nothing here."

"Try the back of the jacket. Maybe he wrote something there."

She peeled the jacket from the book and turned it over. It was blank.

"Face it, Sam. The book is as clean as when it left the store, not even an inscription on a flyleaf. Charlie couldn't have been using it to tell me where I could find a copy of those tax records. The book is just another one of those whimsical gifts he was forever sending me. You heard what Alan Peterman said—how Charlie was always giving him presents that didn't make sense."

Sam shook his head stubbornly. "No, I'm not convinced of that. I think Fowler wanted you to know something, and he used this book to do it."

"Is this just that FBI insight of yours again?"

He didn't answer her. He was silent for a long moment, presumably lost in thought.

"Check the titles of the stories," he urged her. "You never know. Maybe one of them will trigger something."

Hardly likely, she thought, but she humored him, turning to the Table of Contents. "You see, just the usual, classic fairy tales a little girl might enjoy, which he should have realized I stopped being long ago. 'Rumplestiltskin,' 'Cinderella,' 'Sleeping Beauty,' 'Hansel and—'"

She broke off there, seized by a sudden memory. Was it possible?

"What?" Sam demanded.

"I don't know. Maybe…"

"You've got something. Tell me what it is. 'Hansel and Gretel,'" he prompted her.

"I used to collect salt and pepper shakers. I still do."

"And?"

"I must have been about nine years old. Even then I was interested in cooking, and Charlie knew that. I wrote him about it and my collection."

"Go on."

"Well, he sent me this pepper shaker, a ceramic Hansel. There was a note with it. A very sweet note. How he was keeping the Gretel salt shaker for himself, and that way we'd always have a reminder of each other. I still have the Hansel at home."

"And if he hung on to the Gretel all these years—Eve, that's it! It's got to be! Come on, let's find a cab. You and I are going to use that condo key Peterman gave you."

The afternoon was lengthening when the taxi set them down at the address printed on the tag attached to the key. The building, a high-rise, was in one of those affluent areas between Michigan Avenue and the lake. Though not as tall or as grand as its neighbors, it was impressive enough.

Charlie had lived well, Eve thought, gazing up at the building as she climbed out of the taxi. And why not? As Victor DeMarco's accountant, he would have earned an enviable salary.

She hated to think that the man who had been her father, who had been so generous and loving to her through the years, had made his money working for a crime lord. Pointless of her to mind this so much now that he was dead, but she did.

As vigilant as always, Sam had kept a sharp eye through the rear window of the taxi on their way to the condo, making certain there was no suspicious vehicle tailing them. He was just as careful when they emerged from the cab, checking up and down the street before they headed for the entrance.

The building was the kind of place that should have had a doorman, but there was no one on duty. Nor did anyone challenge them when they crossed the lobby to the elevators.

According to the tag on the key, the condo was on the twentieth floor. Sam was silent while they waited for an elevator, and equally quiet as they rode up in the elevator that finally arrived.

Eve wondered if he was occupied with thoughts similar to her own. Like questioning the point of this errand. Things such as Charlie having used such an obscure method to tell her where a copy of the tax records could be located. Trusting her to get that copy to the FBI, if anything happened to him.

It was all so unlikely. Because if the FBI had thoroughly searched the condo, and they would have, they could have already found the copy in whatever form it existed. Or, if not the FBI, then DeMarco's people.

No, she was wrong, Eve decided when they left the elevator. Sam wasn't sharing any of her uncertainties. A quick glance at the resolute expression on his face told her he knew they were in the right place and why.

"This way," he said, after comparing the number on the key she handed him against the numbered doors of the other condos on the floor.

They turned to the left, making their way along a wide, lushly carpeted corridor. Sam halted them in front of the last door.

"Let me have your bag."

Turning the shoulder bag over to him, she watched him withdraw the pistol. Did he think it was possible someone could be lurking in there, waiting to ambush them? Evidently he did, because after returning the bag to her, he nodded toward the door across the hall marked Fire Exit.

"Wait over there while I check out the place," he instructed her. "If you hear anything at all while I'm in there, you get yourself down those stairs to the lobby and out of here."

Obeying him, she stationed herself at the Fire Exit

door as he inserted the key into the lock and disappeared into the condo, the gun stretched out in front of him.

Eve heard no sound from inside the apartment as she waited for Sam to return, but he seemed to be taking an awfully long time. She was beginning to worry about that when he finally reappeared.

"All clear," he reported.

"You were gone so long."

"Took me a while to look for any possible bugs. I didn't find any, and I know all the tricks for concealing them. All the same," he added, spreading the door wide to admit her, "let's keep our voices low while we're in there."

Eve preceded him into the apartment. She hadn't anticipated what Charlie's tastes might be. Maybe something traditional, even old-fashioned. The condo was nothing like that. Its furnishings were extremely modern. Glass-topped tables and highly polished wood, as if the unit had been purchased with everything already in place.

There was an atmosphere of silent abandonment. Eve was immediately aware of it. It saddened her, knowing that the condo's owner would never come here again.

"Everything meticulous," she murmured. "Nothing out of place. I could almost believe the place was never searched."

"Yeah, the FBI team would have been careful about that," Sam said, tucking the pistol into his belt after closing the door. "DeMarco's boys, too, if they managed to get in here, and you can bet they did. Where do we start?"

"The kitchen, I should think. It's the logical place to keep a salt shaker."

Sam led the way through a dining area with tall windows that framed spectacular views of the lake. The kitchen, when they reached it, gleamed with stainless steel fixtures.

They had no need to look through cupboards for the Gretel shaker. The ceramic figure stood in the open on the back of the stove.

"As they say," Sam said, picking up the shaker, "you want to conceal something, you hide it in plain sight." He handed the Gretel to her. "Here, you do the honors."

"The head screws off for refilling." Eve demonstrated by twisting the head, into which holes had been punched for releasing the salt, until it came off into her hand. "Nothing but salt clear up to the top," she reported after looking into the cavity.

"Pour it out on the counter."

If Sam was expecting something buried in the salt, then he had to be disappointed. All that emerged when she tipped the container over was a pile of salt on the granite surface of the counter.

"Check the inside again."

She did as he urged, this time with excitement. "Sam, there's something wrapped in plastic wedged in the bottom! I need a knife to pry it out!"

"Coming up."

He jerked open drawers, found a table knife and passed it to her. Eve inserted the blade into the shaker, dislodging its secret with the tip. What slid out into her waiting hand, even before she unwrapped it, revealed itself through the clear plastic.

"Bingo!" Sam said, seizing the flash drive.

"What now?" she wondered.

"We get this up on a computer, just to make certain it's what it must be."

"Charlie would have had one somewhere in the condo."

"Not anymore. The FBI would have taken any computer away with them—that is, if DeMarco didn't get to it first."

"Then where—?"

"My apartment, my computer."

The taxi, from which Sam had again watched the streets behind them to make sure they weren't being followed, deposited them in front of a four-story building located on Chicago's near North Side. It was a pleasant neighborhood, Eve thought, but there was no question of a doorman this time. This was not the high-rent district.

Unlike his wallet, ID and passport, Sam's keys had been in a pocket of his trousers when the plane burned. One of those keys enabled him to let them into his third-floor apartment, which he checked out before admitting her.

In sharp contrast to Charlie's condo, Sam's apartment had the spare, careless look of a bachelor who didn't mind what his home was like as long as it was comfortable and included a large-screen TV and an oversized lounge chair.

Eve followed him to his computer, which was mounted on his desk at one end of the living room, and stood over him while he powered up the machine and inserted the flash drive. Several files appeared on the screen. Each one was labeled with a specific span of years that, totaled, covered two decades.

Eve could see no other titles on the files, although she leaned over Sam's shoulder to make certain she was missing nothing.

"Uh, would you mind not standing so close?"

She must have been breathing on the back of his ear, something he would have once welcomed, regarding it as an invitation to more intimate activities. But that time was gone. Now her soft breath, stirring the curling tendrils of hair behind his ear, seemed to make him nothing but uneasy. And Eve sad.

"Sorry," she murmured, moving back a few safe inches.

Sam began to open the files one after another, filling the screen.

"It's all here, Eve. Twenty years of Victor DeMarco's tax records."

Not just the tax records, she noted, which might have been useless in themselves, but Charlie's careful explanations of just how and where he had cheated on behalf of the mobster, hiding profits that must have saved DeMarco hundreds of thousands of dollars annually.

Sam was pleased. "There's more than enough evidence here to convict DeMarco of tax fraud. Now," he said, after closing the files and ejecting the flash drive, "I just have to decide where to hide this until that mole is out of the way."

"It wasn't discovered in Charlie's salt shaker. Why not trust it in your own shaker?" she suggested. "Assuming you have one and that it's large enough."

"Perfect. I do, and I think it is." He got up from the desk, but before he led the way into his kitchen he stopped at a front window overlooking the street below.

He's making sure there's no one out there watching the apartment, Eve thought, eyeing him as he stood to one side of the window and peered into the street. He must have been satisfied because he moved on into the kitchen, with Eve close behind him.

His salt shaker, unlike Charlie's Gretel, was an ordinary one but just big enough to accommodate the flash drive. When it had been wrapped again in the plastic cover, squeezed down under the salt and the lid on the container replaced, Sam glanced at the clock on the stove.

"It's too late for me to tackle my squad supervisor. Frank will have left the office by now. I'll have to go into the bureau tomorrow. You hungry? We seem to have missed lunch."

"I could eat."

"Thing is, I don't have anything in the fridge but beer. You up for a delivery pizza? I think we can risk that."

"Fine." She would have told him that, had he the necessary ingredients on hand, she could have made a pizza for them. But, given the barrier he was maintaining, it seemed too familiar a confidence.

Forty minutes later, seated across from each other at his kitchen table, with frosty cans of beer in front of them and the pizza between them, they satisfied their appetites with the slices gooey with cheese while Michael Bublé entertained them on Sam's CD player.

At least we're sharing this much, Eve thought. Except that while it might look cozy, it didn't feel cozy. There was an underlying tension in the room that had as much to do with the intimacy of her presence in his apartment as it did with his perpetual caution about her safety. His visits to the front windows at regular intervals was evidence of that.

"You can't go with me tomorrow," he said after they'd finished the pizza. "They'd take you into custody. I don't like the idea of leaving you, but you'll have to stay here."

Yes, she had already realized she would have to hide out until the mole was caught. Which meant spending the night in his apartment. Maybe several nights. A necessity she didn't relish.

Did he recognize the temptations in that arrangement? Was that why he added a quick "There's a spare bedroom you can have. Has its own bathroom, even clean sheets on the bed. I never use it."

She nodded and rose from the table to clear away the remains of their meal. "I think I'll have a bath before I turn in for the night."

She left him with the impression she was casual about the whole thing when she was anything but. The bath should have relaxed her, but she couldn't seem to get comfortable when she climbed into bed.

The mattress wasn't responsible for the restless night she spent. The man in the next room was. She was far too conscious of his being on the other side of the wall away from her.

She kept picturing him in his own bed. Somehow she didn't think Sam would be clad in pajamas, and wondered if he slept in the nude, as he had back at the cabin. An image of him lying there like that, all hard muscle and warm, musky skin, had her damning her treacherous imagination.

The maddening thing in the end wasn't his body, arousing as it was. It was having fallen in love with the man who had surfaced without a memory to haunt him. The Sam McDonough who could be funny and sensitive and strong, embodying all the best qualities of his sex.

If that decent, caring man had existed before Lily's death, then he must still be there under all the dark anguish. But for all her efforts, all her yearning, she couldn't manage to reach him.

When Eve finally did fall asleep, she paid the price by being troubled by a series of erotic dreams. All of them with her naked and eager in Sam's arms.

Chapter 13

Sam wanted his meeting with his squad supervisor to be as businesslike as possible. Which was why he was dressed in the dark suit, which seemed to be the standard uniform of an FBI special agent, when he rapped on Eve's door the next morning.

What she wore when she finally answered his knock came close to robbing him of his self-control. He must have left one of his old shirts in the closet of the guest bedroom, and she had borrowed it to sleep in. And, unless she had panties and a bra on underneath, and he preferred to think she didn't, this was all she was wearing as she stood framed there in the doorway.

He caught his breath at the sexy sight of her, bare legs extending their shapely length from the hem of the shirt, hair tousled, face flushed from sleep.

Damn!

Looking like that, she reignited what had taken all

his willpower last night to extinguish. The flaming urge to leave his bed, charge into her room and slide into bed beside her.

Now he had to manage a steady "I've got coffee made, and I found some frozen waffles in the freezer. Until I can shop for groceries, that's all we have for breakfast."

"Give me ten minutes," was all she said before closing the door on him.

Sam was relieved when she appeared in the kitchen in the trim slacks and top she had bought at one of the discount stores along their route. She was still desirable, even fully dressed.

"I've been thinking about leaving you here alone," he said over the coffee and waffles. "It's no good. If anyone should come looking for you, this is the first place they'll try."

They hadn't so far. He'd been faithful about periodically checking the street. All the same...

Eve shook her head. "There isn't enough money left for anything like a hotel room."

"Not necessary. I've got the perfect hideaway for you. The apartment across the hall. I have the key to it on my ring."

"How did that happen?" she asked, reaching for the coffeepot to refill her mug.

"The guy who lives there is overseas for a couple of months. He left a key with me in case of emergency. I don't think he was figuring on exactly this kind of emergency, but I'm going to think of it as one."

When their simple breakfast had been cleared away, Sam escorted Eve across the hall and into the other apartment. It had the same layout as his. Except, he admitted to himself, it was a lot better furnished.

"Will you be all right here?" he asked her after he had looked over the rooms. Just to be sure.

"Why shouldn't I be?"

"No reason. I guess I don't need to tell you to keep the door locked. And if anyone should come knocking, which they won't, not to answer it. Same for the phone. And, uh, stay away from the windows. Better not turn on the TV or radio, either." He glanced around the living room. Unlike his own apartment, there were plenty of books in evidence. "Maybe you can find one of these books to read."

"Uh-huh."

He gazed at her standing there, her bag still over her shoulder. *She isn't happy about this,* he thought. He wasn't, either, but what else could he do?

"I'll leave the pistol here with you." He laid the gun on the coffee table.

"I hope you don't expect me to use it."

"If I thought there was any chance of that, I wouldn't leave you here on your own. It's just a precaution. Also, I don't want to show up with it at the bureau. They kind of frown on a special agent carrying a weapon that hasn't been officially issued to him."

"Understood."

"Look, don't worry if I'm not back for a few hours. I don't how long this thing with Kowsloski is going to take. When I do get away, I'll need to stop at my bank to withdraw some cash, after which I'll shop for groceries."

"Anything else?"

"I guess not."

"Then you'd better go."

He went, but not until he heard the sound of Eve locking the door behind him did Sam head for the elevator. On his way down, he made a mental note to swing by

Union Station sometime this morning to collect those coats from the locker.

His Mustang was parked where he had left it in one of the coveted spots near the entrance to his building. His long absence had cost him a busted headlight, which he had unhappily noticed when the cab had dropped them off yesterday at the front of the building. Right now it was the least of his concerns.

Just before climbing behind the wheel of the Mustang, he glanced up at one of the windows of his neighbor's apartment. Eve was up there out of sight. He told himself he had no reason to worry about her.

Hell, McDonough, she isn't a child. She's a capable woman able to take care of herself. She doesn't need you hovering over her.

It was a good argument. Now he just had to convince himself to believe it.

The Chicago division of the FBI was located on Roosevelt Road in a tall building that was more glass than solid walls.

Sam plugged the Mustang into a slot in the adjoining parking lot, locked it and strode toward the entrance.

The security in the lobby was tight. But, even though his shield and ID had gone up in smoke back in Canada, he had no trouble getting past the desk. Not only was he a familiar face to the guards, he wore his picture tag fixed to the lapel of his suit coat that hadn't gone with him to Canada.

One of the elevators carried him to an upper floor where his department was located. News had to have traveled through the ranks that he was missing and there had been no contact from him, because heads turned as Sam made his way through the bull pen toward his squad supervisor's office. But only one of the special agents spoke to him.

The gum-chewing Whit Cooper popped up from his cubicle with a loud "You're back! Man, have we been worried about you!"

Everything Whit did was loud, and sometimes obnoxious. Not that Sam had anything against him. Whit just thought he was being funny. He wasn't.

The only other agent who acknowledged his return with a wave of welcome and a boyish grin of pleasure was Bud Lowry. Sam liked Bud, flaming hair, freckles and all. He was a good agent.

Although he and Bud weren't exactly close, they did hang out together on occasion, which was why he hated to ignore the guy. But a meeting with Kowsloski was a priority.

Without breaking his stride, Sam returned the wave with a silently mouthed "Later," promising himself he would stop by Bud's desk on his way out.

Frank was on the phone when Sam arrived at his office. The squad supervisor faced the window, his back to the open door. Kowsloski had the uncanny ability to sense when one of his agents appeared in his private domain. Unless the wave of excitement out in the bull pen had alerted him, that was true now.

Either way, he swiveled around in his chair behind his desk. There was no expression on his round face when he discovered Sam standing there just inside the door.

"I'll have to call you back," he said to whoever was on the other end of the line. Placing the phone back in its cradle, he addressed Sam with a calm "You okay?"

"Don't I look okay?"

"Yeah, you do." Then both his expression and his tone sharply altered, his fleshy face going a livid red, his voice rising from flat to a roar. "Then why the hell didn't you contact me? And where is Eve Warren?"

"In a safe place here in the city."

Voices carried, maybe to the wrong ears. Aware of that, Sam closed the office door behind him before he approached Frank's desk. Hands planted on its surface, he leaned toward the squad supervisor.

"Are you going to go on blasting me, or do you want to hear what's happened since you sent me off to the Yukon?"

"I know what happened. You and Eve Warren went down in a plane in the wilderness. The one and only report I got from Canada, with no word since then, was that the wreckage was never sighted."

"Not by the authorities up there, but DeMarco's boys had no trouble finding us. They were the ones who forced the plane down. You interested in the rest?"

"I'm listening, but you'd better make me like what I hear. If not, you could be sweeping floors out there in the bull pen instead of carrying a badge."

Sam launched into his story, telling Kowsloski everything he needed to know as concisely as possible, starting with his arrival in the Yukon and ending with his and Eve's return to Chicago and their discovery of the flash drive.

Frank was silent for a moment after Sam's plea to him to enlist Internal Affairs in finding and taking down the mole. Was the squad supervisor convinced that a mole did exist? Sam didn't learn that. All he finally got from Kowsloski was a quiet, deadly "I want that flash drive, McDonough."

"You don't get it, or where I've stashed Eve Warren, until the mole is out of the way."

"You know what you're risking here, don't you?"

"Yeah, I know. Trading in my career for that broom."

From the time he had opened those tax files on his computer, Sam had considered turning the flash drive over to his squad supervisor. It was all Frank wanted, needed. But that wouldn't guarantee Eve's safety. As long as the mole was active, feeding DeMarco information, she was in danger.

The mobster was unpredictable. If he was led to believe that Eve had knowledge of his activities beyond the existence of those tax records, could testify against him, he was capable of ordering a hit on her.

No, Sam wouldn't take that chance. He had taken a chance with Lily, and look how that had turned out. Withholding the flash drive was his only leverage, his only way to protect Eve until the mole was revealed.

He stood erect, leaning away from the desk. "Well?"

Frank muttered a reluctant, "I'll get Internal Affairs on it. But I warn you, McDonough, if this thing backfires, I'm gonna have your ass."

Sam remembered his promise to himself to stop by Bud Lowry's desk when he came away from the squad supervisor's office. But Bud was no longer in his pod. He spoke to Lowry's neighbor, another special agent, on the other side of the divider.

"Angie, you know where Bud went?"

She seemed to be engrossed in a report she was writing on her computer. Looking up from her work, she tossed Sam a brief "He had a dentist appointment for a tooth that's been giving him trouble all week."

That was when Sam noticed that her other neighbor, Whit Cooper, was also no longer on the scene. "Where's Whit?"

"Dunno. He mumbled something about an errand and just took off."

"Thanks. Tell Bud when he returns that I'll catch him later."

It wasn't until Sam was going down in the elevator that, for no reason he could name, he began to have an uneasy feeling about Whit Cooper's sudden, swift departure from his desk. That feeling escalated when he reached the lobby.

Was it possible? No, that was crazy. He was being paranoid. Obnoxious or not, Whit had too clean a record to be Victor DeMarco's paid informant.

All right, so maybe just before he had closed Frank's office door, the guy might have overheard Sam's assurance to their squad supervisor that he'd put Eve in a safe place. It didn't make Whit Cooper the mole, not when other agents in the bull pen could have heard the same thing.

All the same, his suspicion persisted as he exited the building and headed rapidly toward his car. No motive, he tried to tell himself. Whit had no motive to turn informer. Unless…

He remembered something about Whit. Something potentially damning. Cooper had a gambling habit. Or did have, because a couple of weeks ago he claimed to have cured himself. But what if that was a lie? What if Whit was so steeped in gaming debts he'd been willing to feed DeMarco information in exchange for sums he badly needed? Even perform other favors for the mobster?

It was only speculation, not evidence. Not enough to alert Frank Kowsloski and maybe harm the reputation of a solid agent.

But it was enough to send Sam speeding out of the

parking lot with a sense of deepening urgency he couldn't seem to shake, even though he tried to tell himself Eve couldn't be in danger. Whit wouldn't have the remotest idea where she was.

That was what Sam convinced himself. Until on his way to his apartment building he remembered something else that made him sick with dread. Whit *knew* he had the key to that other apartment.

Sam and Bud Lowry sometimes engaged in a game of handball after work. A few weeks back, Bud had accompanied him home so Sam could change clothes for the court. Whit Cooper, although uninvited, had ended up tagging along with them. He'd witnessed Sam trying to fit the wrong key into his door, listened to him mutter an explanation of why he had the almost identical key to the apartment across the hall on his ring.

Whit Cooper would have guessed where he could find Eve Warren!

That certainty had Sam breaking every traffic law in his need to get back to Eve. Praying all the way he would reach her in time. In time for what he wouldn't allow himself to consider. But if that SOB put his hands on her...

He caught a break when he reached his building. The parking space he had vacated was still open. A miracle. Not that he would have hesitated to double-park in the street.

He didn't wait for the elevator. He used the stairs, knowing as he raced up to his floor that Cooper would have had no trouble getting into his neighbor's apartment. All Whit would have had to do was hunt up the building super, flash his FBI credentials and the super would have unlocked the door for him.

A result that was confirmed when Sam reached the

door and found it ajar. His fear overriding his caution, he smacked the door wide open to total silence.

The first thing he noticed was the absence of the pistol from the coffee table where he had placed it. The second was Eve's empty bag on the floor, its contents strewn across the carpet.

Gone! Cooper had taken her away. But where and how long ago?

Needing to make certain the place was deserted, that Cooper wasn't holding Eve in one of the other rooms, Sam made a swift tour of the apartment.

He had reached the second, smaller bedroom. Was squeezing his way past the king-sized bed and the wall toward a bathroom when, forced to turn sideways in order to navigate the narrow space, he found it necessary to steady himself with a hand on the ledge of the window there. That was how he discovered it in the alley below at the side of the building.

A dark green SUV facing out toward the street. He recognized the vehicle with a jolt of disbelief. It belonged not to Whit Cooper but to Bud Lowry. Lowry was down there now, and he wasn't alone. He had Eve with him. Was forcing her at gunpoint to slide behind the wheel of the SUV.

The pistol. Lowry was using the pistol he had helped himself to from the coffee table, not the FBI weapon issued to him. A weapon whose bullets could be traced back to him if he had to shoot his captive.

Not Eve! He couldn't lose Eve as he had lost Lily! It would kill him if that happened.

He had no time to wonder why his friend had turned mole. All that mattered was Eve. Gut churning with a desperate promise to himself to save the woman he so reluctantly loved, fiercely denying that love to himself even now, Sam sped out of the apartment and along the hall to the stairway. The stairway he must have been climbing at the same time Lowry was taking Eve down in the elevator and out a side door to the alley.

There was no sign of the SUV when he reached the street. It would have fled the alley by now with a terrified Eve at the wheel. Going where? Sam asked himself as he sprinted toward the Mustang. He still didn't know. Not until he was tearing recklessly up the one-way street in pursuit, anyway. And then he had a pretty good idea of Lowry's destination.

Eve had a terrible feeling she was going to be delivered to Victor DeMarco. Used as a hostage in exchange for the incriminating tax records. Or worse.

She had tried to confirm that, but her captor refused to tell her anything, including his identity. He wouldn't, of course, although she could guess. Whoever he was, he wore the same dark, conservative suit Sam had worn when he'd left her in the apartment. The uniform of an FBI special agent. The mole who had betrayed them? Had to be.

How he had found her in that apartment—taken her by surprise, while she was stretched out on the sofa in an effort to catch up on her lost sleep of last night—was another mystery. Not that it mattered. All that did matter was how frightened she was, scarcely able to manage the SUV as they wove through the streets.

"Do you have to keep that gun trained on me? You're making me nervous. You don't want us to get into an accident, do you?"

"Shut up and drive," he snarled. "Take the next turn left."

Eve did as he directed. What other choice did she have?

A moment later she found herself blending in with the traffic on a freeway that seemed to be headed in a northerly direction. She was used to driving in big-city traffic in St. Louis. But Chicago traffic was murder. It needed all her concentration.

Maybe that's why it took her a while to notice it behind them in the rearview mirror. A sporty, silver Mustang. Not just any silver Mustang, either. This one had a broken headlamp. The left one.

Sam! It had to be Sam back there!

She remembered him complaining about the headlight when the taxi had dropped them off in front of his building yesterday. Remembered him grumbling, "Probably kids playing ball again in the street when they've got a park just a half block over."

It couldn't be anything but Sam's silver Mustang. How long had he been following them? As far back as somewhere in that maze of streets before the freeway? If so, she hadn't been aware of him. Not when she'd been so worried, wondering if she would have any opportunity to get away from her captor before they reached their destination. Because once they got there, there would be no chance for an escape.

But now there was Sam speeding to her rescue on a— well, with a silver charger under him, if not a white one. Providing, that is, he could keep them in sight. And that was a problem. The traffic was thickening, with other vehicles squeezing between the Mustang and the SUV.

There were tense moments when she lost sight of the Mustang in her rearview mirror. To her relief, it always appeared again, either directly behind them or a few car lengths back in one of the other lanes.

But how long could Sam continue to follow the SUV before it disappeared on him altogether? Unless...

Easing her pressure on the accelerator, Eve slowed the SUV, letting it drop back.

"What are you doing?" her red-haired captor demanded.

Her effort was a mistake. He'd been too busy holding the gun on her, watching her every move, to check the traffic behind them. But if she made him suspicious...

"Just trying not to hit the car in front of me."

"Get over to the right, and you won't. And keep your speed up."

She obeyed him while searching her mind for some other way to help Sam. Her captor gave it to her when they'd traveled another half mile or so up the highway.

"We're going to leave the freeway on the exit after the next one. Get over to the outside lane so you're ready for it."

Eve did as she was instructed. Only it wasn't the second exit that she made her target. It was the first one.

"Not here!" her captor screamed at her when she aimed the SUV down the off-ramp. "The next one! I told you the next one!"

"Stop shouting at me. You're confusing me."

"Get us back on the freeway. *Now.*"

Had her ruse worked? She flashed a glance in the rearview mirror. There was no sign of Sam. All she could do now was attempt another delay. Hope he would catch up to them.

"Where are you going? This isn't the way to the on-ramp!"

"The way you keep yelling at me, why wouldn't I miss it? I'll have to find a place to turn around."

"Then you'd better find it, and find it fast!"

What she found after they'd traveled another block along the street was a narrow alley. One that was blocked less than halfway along its length by a large trash receptacle. Eve didn't hesitate to swing into it.

"You stupid bitch! You've got us into a dead end with nowhere to turn! Back out!"

Too late for that. The Mustang arrived, sliding into the alley behind them. And this time the man at her side was fully aware of it.

Eve felt the barrel of the pistol jammed into her side.

"Get out," he commanded her. "And don't try to make a run for it, unless you want a bullet in your back."

With trembling hands, she unbuckled her seat belt, opened the door and exited the SUV. The pistol remained in her side as he scooted under the wheel directly behind her.

Sam was out of his car, not daring to approach them. Watching them carefully as her captor shifted the gun in his hand to the back of her head, wrapped his other arm tightly around her waist and backed them up against the trash receptacle.

"I'll shoot her, Sam, if you don't let us out of here. I swear I will."

His voice low and even, but with steel behind every word, Sam answered him with a confident "No, you won't. It's over, Bud. You're finished. Be smart and let her go. You can cut a deal if you cooperate. Probably spend a few years behind bars, maybe shorten your sentence with good behavior."

"You're forgetting who's holding the gun here."

"Or," Sam continued, as if he hadn't heard the other man, "you can make the kind of mistake that will cost you a lifetime in prison."

"Not if I kill both of you and leave you in this alley. No witnesses, Sam."

"But you won't do that. Hear those sirens, Bud? See, when I came chasing down off that ramp it was at top speed. Made sure a police cruiser saw that, too. The cops think they're after me, but when they get here and it's all sorted out, it's you they'll be hauling off in handcuffs."

Sam wasn't bluffing. The sirens were louder now, heralding their approach. There was a taut silence of indecision in the alley itself. It probably lasted for only seconds, but seemed much longer than that to Eve before she felt the pistol swing away from her, heard it clatter on the pavement, experienced the relief of her captor releasing her.

She was conscious by then of the flashing blue and red lights of the cruiser and its backup in the mouth of the alley, the banging of car doors. Only dimly so, however, since her awareness was more fully occupied with an effort to keep herself from collapsing now that she no longer had the support, welcome or not, of the man called Bud.

Her legs must have been visibly sagging, because Sam was suddenly there, his arms wrapping around her. His strong, protective embrace felt wonderful, even though Eve knew this could be the last time she would experience it.

Chapter 14

Eve was amazed at the speed and efficiency of the FBI when it swung into action, as it did within minutes of their arrival at the Chicago division.

Eve was led to an office by one of the special agents who introduced herself as Angela Carter. Although the woman, who looked more like a runway model than an agent, was sympathetic, she wanted every detail, rapidly taking each of them down on a computer.

The interview was so lengthy and exacting that Eve had no time to wonder what had become of Sam. Maybe he was relating his own version of today's events in another area, most likely having reported all the rest earlier to his squad supervisor.

When they were finished, Agent Carter printed out the interview, gave it to Eve to read and asked her to sign it.

"Our supervisory special agent asked to see you when we were done," the woman told her. "If you'll come this way…"

Eve was led across the common area to another office where she was introduced to Frank Kowsloski, who rose from his desk and came forward to shake her hand.

"On behalf of the FBI, Miss Warren, I want to express my gratitude for your help. Will you take a chair, please? I think you're entitled to know what's been happening since Special Agent McDonough handed you over to Special Agent Carter."

Sam was there in the office, too, half seated, half leaning on a low window ledge, his arms folded across his chest. There was nothing on his chiseled face that told her what he might be thinking or feeling. All he said to her was, "You okay, Eve?"

She nodded and seated herself in one of the chairs, prepared to listen to the squad supervisor, who had returned to his desk.

In the half hour that followed, while aware of Sam's steady gaze on her, Eve heard more than she probably needed or wanted to know.

Information like how the flash drive and what it contained, together with Bud Lowry's full confession and willingness to testify at Victor DeMarco's trial, had convinced the federal prosecutor that the mobster would serve a long stretch in prison.

Also, how, the bureau had been in contact with Canadian authorities, who were ready to handle everything at that end regarding the bodies of DeMarco's two thugs. The FBI was promising to reimburse the owners of the cabin, who turned out to be a pair of brothers from Winnipeg, for any loss or damage.

She was even told Bud Lowry's motive for turning informant. It was a simple, all-too-common one. Lowry had a girlfriend he was wild about. A woman who had expensive tastes. Far too expensive to support on an agent's salary. Taking huge sums from DeMarco in exchange for information had been the result.

None of it really interested Eve. The only question she had for the squad supervisor was a concerned "What about Ken Redfeather, our pilot?"

"His remains will be located and returned to his family," she was assured.

"What happens to me now?"

"There'll be a warrant for Victor DeMarco's arrest, although I'm afraid it's too late in the day for a judge to issue it. Which is why I'm placing you overnight in a downtown hotel under the protection of Agents McDonough and Carter. I won't consider you safe, Miss Warren, until both DeMarco and his lawyer are made fully aware of the evidence we have that no longer depends on you in any way."

Eve was too exhausted by then to either question or object to Frank Kowsloski's decision. Nor, once they were settled in that hotel room, was there any opportunity for a private conversation with Sam. Not with the constant presence of Special Agent Carter.

Had Sam wanted it this way? She didn't know.

When she turned in early for the night, it was with a sorrowful acceptance of everything she wanted and feared she wouldn't get.

Why did I have to go and fall in love with you, Sam McDonough?

Frank Kowsloski appeared in the hotel room just after noon the next day to cheerfully tell her, "You're free to go, Miss Warren. Victor DeMarco has been arrested and charged. He won't be a threat to you any more."

"Will you need me to testify at his trial?"

"I don't see that as necessary, not with all the evidence we have. But we can always contact you later on, if it turns out you're needed. Meanwhile, I'm sure Agent McDonough here will be happy to take you where you want to go."

Eve wasn't so sure about that. The mood between Sam and her had become awkward. He didn't hesitate to take charge, though, when they left the hotel. "We'll go back to my apartment, maybe grab some lunch on the way."

He had already recovered her shoulder bag and its contents last night, bringing them to her in the hotel after stopping by Union Station to retrieve their coats. He'd also stopped by a cash machine to withdraw some funds. Eve had no reason to return to Sam's apartment. There was nothing there for her now.

There never had been, she thought sadly.

Was it her imagination that Sam seemed relieved when she declined his suggestion?

"Where then?" he asked her.

"Since you're offering, I'd appreciate it if you drove me to Charlie's condo."

Though he didn't ask her why, the look on his face expressed surprise.

She answered his curiosity with a casual "I want to pick up the Gretel salt shaker. Alan Peterman could see no objection to my taking it away from the condo when I phoned him last night while you were running your errands. It's all I want from the place."

"Planning on reuniting it with your Hansel?"

Eve nodded. "Sappy sentiment, I suppose, but I'd like something of Charlie's that has a happy association for me."

They didn't talk on the drive north. The atmosphere between them was still strained. Sam dropped her off at the entrance to Charlie's building.

"No parking on the street here," he said. "I'll have to find a lot or a parking garage. You can wait for me in the lobby."

"That might take too long. I have the key. I can go up and let myself in."

Before he could object, she was out of the Mustang and on her way to the elevators. By the time he rejoined her, she was back in the lobby, bearing the Gretel.

"Lunch now?" he asked her.

Eve drew a deep breath and exhaled it slowly in an effort to find the courage she suddenly knew she needed. It was time, wasn't it? Time to confront him with what he probably didn't want to hear but what she was determined to communicate before they parted. That much she deserved.

"I don't want to go to lunch. I don't want to go anywhere with you, Sam. There's just no point to it."

He frowned, looking puzzled. "What are you talking about?"

"I think you already know. I think you've known for a long time. You just don't want to admit it."

He stared at her, either genuinely confused or pretending to be. "You're not making sense. And this is one time those eyebrows of yours...well, they aren't telling me anything."

"Us, Sam. You and me. You have to have realized I'm in love with you. And if you imagine that was easy for me to say, it wasn't."

"Eve—"

"No, just hear me out, because I feel maybe you could be in love with me. But you won't let yourself admit that, either, will you? After Lily, you're afraid of any commitment."

He was silent, suddenly hard to read. But there was

something in his eyes that suggested to her his emotions were at war with each other. And that this terrible conflict was making him deeply unhappy. She should have cared about that. But she didn't. She refused to let any of it stop her. It was time he heard the stark truth.

"Sometimes, Sam, I think you actually enjoy being sunk in your own misery, that you don't want anyone trying to help you overcome that fear that's holding you hostage."

"That's enough," he told her, his voice husky.

"Not yet. There's one more thing. *Do* you love me, Sam? Can you tell me that much?"

He couldn't. He could only go on gazing at her, his eyes pleading for her not to press him any further. This time she took pity on him. Took pity on both of them, because she was suffering, too. She had gambled again and lost.

"All right, Sam. I'm finished now. I won't bother you anymore. I'm going."

"Where?"

"Back home. That's another thing I did last night. I called Union Station. There's a train to St. Louis this afternoon. I should just be able to make it."

"I'll get the car."

She shook her head. "I prefer to hail a cab."

He stopped her as she started for the entrance. "You can't have enough money left for a train ticket. Let me—"

"I don't need any cash. You forget, it's safe for me to use my credit cards now."

She didn't want any goodbyes. Didn't want the risk of tears. Which was why, hurting though she was, she simply walked away, leaving him there in the lobby alone.

* * *

A numbness stealing over him, Sam watched her through the glass doors emerge on the sidewalk. She didn't have to find a taxi. He was vaguely conscious of a cab arriving at the front entrance of the building to discharge three passengers.

Eve claimed the taxi before it could pull away. Seconds later the cab was gone, carrying Eve with it and out of his life.

Sam welcomed the mindlessness that continued to hold him in its grip as he found his way out onto the sidewalk, knowing it was the only way he could get through this thing. But somewhere under the haze that carried him toward the parking garage where he had left the Mustang, he became slowly aware of the hollowness inside him. As if something essential to his existence had been severed from his body, and he was just now beginning to feel the loss.

He had yet to reach the garage when he halted on the sidewalk, the fog suddenly lifting, defeated by a clarity that would no longer be ignored. Leaving him stricken with the realization of his stubborn, blind stupidity.

Eve had been right. She had been right about everything. He *was* a coward, unwilling to conquer his demons. Unable to let someone matter to him, too fearful of another loss like the one he had endured when Lily died.

Someone like Eve, who was smart, strong and not afraid to challenge him on every level. Who had everything he needed to make him whole again. Because Eve completed him as poor Lily never had, never could.

Dear God, why hadn't he let himself see that? Why had he waited until now to freely, honestly understand he was the right man for her? That he didn't just love her, as he had already realized days ago, but that, unlike what he'd felt for Lily, this was a love that was certain, vital in its intensity.

Eve Warren is the best thing that ever happened to you, and you're letting her get away.

The hell he would!

Minutes later, risking another police pursuit, this time an unwanted one, Sam sped toward Union Station. Praying all the way he would reach the station before that train left for St. Louis. That he could convince her he was ready to risk his heart again.

He had no memory when he got there of just where he parked the car, not caring if it was in an illegal zone. It didn't matter. Only Eve mattered, he thought as he raced into the station.

Union Station was a vast cavern of different levels, track platforms, refreshment counters and other assorted areas whose purposes he didn't know and didn't care about. Finding Eve in this frustrating maze was all that counted.

He paused only long enough to consult one of the monitors listing arrivals and departures. To his relief, the train for St. Louis had yet to be boarded. He still had time, but the minutes were counting down as he hunted for Eve. Where was she in all this thick, rushing traffic that seemed to frustrate him at every turn?

Sam was in a state of near panic when he finally located her in a small, obscure waiting room where the travelers had congregated, waiting to be called to the St. Louis gate. His heart turned over at the welcome sight of her. He hadn't lost her yet. *Wouldn't* lose her if his fierce determination prevailed, and he meant to see that it did.

Eve was parked on a lonely bench in the far corner, looking forlorn and at the same time incredibly sexy.

Squaring his shoulders, Sam approached the bench. She was gazing into space, unaware of his arrival until he loomed directly over her. Only then, with a startled expression, was she conscious of his presence.

"Sam! What are you doing here?"

"Hoping to convince you not to board that train."

"I thought we already had this conversation."

"That was then. This is now."

Her bag, coat and the Gretel shaker rested on the bench beside her. Sam moved them off to the side, making space for himself. Without waiting for an invitation she might refuse if he gave her the opportunity, he joined her on the bench, squeezing in beside her.

She didn't object, didn't try to slide away. He was ready to read that much as encouraging.

She turned to face him, a clear challenge in her voice. "And just what could have changed so suddenly between then and now?"

"Me. I've changed." He paused briefly to regroup. "No, that's not right. I didn't change suddenly and all out of nowhere. That happened a long time ago back at the border, maybe even before then. As you said, I just refused to admit it. Not until after you walked away from me in that damn lobby."

A warning look crept into her steady gaze. "Sam, I can't take any more disappointments. I just can't. And if that's what this turns out to be—"

"It won't," he promised, leaning toward her earnestly. "I won't let it be that way again. For either of us."

He reached for her hands, hoping she wouldn't try to withdraw them when he clasped them between his own. To his relief, she didn't.

"Eve, listen to me, I've come to my senses. It took your

walking out on me to make me realize what an idiot I've been. Just how wrong I was."

He went on to tell her what he'd suffered when she left him in the lobby. How afterwards on the street he'd realized that, if he lost her, he'd be losing his soul.

"I knew what I felt for you long before that," he confessed. "But I was also convinced that you didn't deserve someone like me. And now…well, now I think that I could be right for you. No, that I *am* right for you. That we're right for each other."

Sam was making every effort to win her back, but he couldn't be sure that effort was working. She listened to him without comment, her head tipped to one side. Was it skepticism he read in her eyes? It scared the hell out of him.

Tightening his hands on hers, he doubled his effort. "Eve, with your help I know I can lick the demons that have kept us apart. With you beside me, I can do anything." He ended his plea with what he feared was a lame "That is, if you'll have me."

There was a long silence.

"Eve, say something. You're killing me here."

"Is that all?"

"What more do you want? Name it."

"Sam, there's only one thing I've ever wanted from you. And I don't have it. Yet."

"What—" He broke off with sudden understanding. She didn't have to say it. He knew what she needed to hear. With his heart swelling, he could feel a slow grin spread across his face. A grin of vast relief.

"Yeah?" he said. "My telling you just how much I love you?"

"That would help."

"Then you have it. I love you, Eve Warren. Love you so much it makes me crazy wanting you. Satisfied?"

"Not quite."

If she was asking him to prove it, he was more than ready to do so. And he did. Freeing his hands from hers in order to wind his arms around her, he drew her up against him and kissed her.

It wasn't enough. Not caring what stares in the room might be directed their way, he hauled her up on his lap. Only then could he deliver the kiss he wanted. A kiss that was both tender and fierce at the same time, with the deepest love he was able to convey. To his joy, she smiled when he finally lifted his mouth from hers.

"So what do we do now, Sam?"

In no hurry to release her, he was thoughtful as he continued to cradle her on his lap. "I guess," he said, "I'd better find out what the chances are for an opening in the St. Louis division."

"Yes, you could do that. Or…"

"What?"

"I could think about opening that restaurant I've always wanted here in Chicago."

"We'll figure it out. Home is wherever we both are. Together, angel."

"You called me *angel*. I've missed that."

"You'll hear it a lot from now on."

"I'll count on that, Special Agent McDonough. Let's say for, oh, the rest of our lives."

* * * * *

SUSPENSE

Heartstopping stories of intrigue and mystery—
where true love always triumphs.

COMING NEXT MONTH
AVAILABLE FEBRUARY 28, 2012

#1695 OPERATION MIDNIGHT
Cutter's Code
Justine Davis

#1696 A DAUGHTER'S PERFECT SECRET
Perfect, Wyoming
Kimberly Van Meter

#1697 HIGH-STAKES AFFAIR
Stealth Knights
Gail Barrett

#1698 DEADLY RECKONING
Elle James

REQUEST YOUR FREE BOOKS!
2 FREE NOVELS PLUS 2 FREE GIFTS!

 Harlequin®

ROMANTIC
SUSPENSE

Sparked by Danger, Fueled by Passion.

YES! Please send me 2 FREE Harlequin® Romantic Suspense novels and my 2 FREE gifts (gifts are worth about $10). After receiving them, if I don't wish to receive any more books, I can return the shipping statement marked "cancel." If I don't cancel, I will receive 4 brand-new novels every month and be billed just $4.49 per book in the U.S. or $5.24 per book in Canada. That's a saving of at least 14% off the cover price! It's quite a bargain! Shipping and handling is just 50¢ per book in the U.S. and 75¢ per book in Canada.* I understand that accepting the 2 free books and gifts places me under no obligation to buy anything. I can always return a shipment and cancel at any time. Even if I never buy another book, the two free books and gifts are mine to keep forever.

240/340 HDN FEFR

Name	(PLEASE PRINT)

Address	Apt. #

City	State/Prov.	Zip/Postal Code

Signature (if under 18, a parent or guardian must sign)

Mail to the **Reader Service:**

IN U.S.A.: P.O. Box 1867, Buffalo, NY 14240-1867
IN CANADA: P.O. Box 609, Fort Erie, Ontario L2A 5X3

Not valid for current subscribers to Harlequin Romantic Suspense books.

Want to try two free books from another line?
Call 1-800-873-8635 or visit www.ReaderService.com.

* Terms and prices subject to change without notice. Prices do not include applicable taxes. Sales tax applicable in N.Y. Canadian residents will be charged applicable taxes. Offer not valid in Quebec. This offer is limited to one order per household. All orders subject to credit approval. Credit or debit balances in a customer's account(s) may be offset by any other outstanding balance owed by or to the customer. Please allow 4 to 6 weeks for delivery. Offer available while quantities last.

Your Privacy—The Reader Service is committed to protecting your privacy. Our Privacy Policy is available online at www.ReaderService.com or upon request from the Reader Service.

We make a portion of our mailing list available to reputable third parties that offer products we believe may interest you. If you prefer that we not exchange your name with third parties, or if you wish to clarify or modify your communication preferences, please visit us at www.ReaderService.com/consumerschoice or write to us at Reader Service Preference Service, P.O. Box 9062, Buffalo, NY 14269. Include your complete name and address.

HRS11B

New York Times *and* USA TODAY *bestselling author*
Maya Banks presents book three in her miniseries
PREGNANCY & PASSION.

TEMPTED BY HER INNOCENT KISS

Available March 2012 from Harlequin Desire!

There came a time in a man's life when he knew he was well and truly caught. Devon Carter stared down at the diamond ring nestled in velvet and acknowledged that this was one such time. He snapped the lid closed and shoved the box into the breast pocket of his suit.

He had two choices. He could marry Ashley Copeland and fulfill his goal of merging his company with Copeland Hotels, thus creating the largest, most exclusive line of resorts in the world, or he could refuse and lose it all.

Put in that light, there wasn't much he could do except pop the question.

The doorman to his Manhattan high-rise apartment hurried to open the door as Devon strode toward the street. He took a deep breath before ducking into his car, and the driver pulled into traffic.

Tonight was the night. All of his careful wooing, the countless dinners, kisses that started brief and casual and became more breathless—all a lead-up to tonight. Tonight his seduction of Ashley Copeland would be complete, and then he'd ask her to marry him.

He shook his head as the absurdity of the situation hit him for the hundredth time. Personally, he thought William Copeland was crazy for forcing his daughter down Devon's throat.

Ashley was a sweet enough girl, but Devon had no desire

to marry anyone.

William had other plans. He'd told Devon that Ashley had no head for the family business. She was too softhearted, too naive. So he'd made Ashley part of the deal. The catch? Ashley wasn't to know of it. Which meant Devon was stuck playing stupid games.

Ashley was supposed to think this was a grand love match. She was a starry-eyed woman who preferred her animal-rescue foundation over board meetings, charts and financials for Copeland Hotels.

If she ever found out the truth, she wouldn't take it well.

And hell, he couldn't blame her.

But no matter the reason for his proposal, before the night was over, she'd have no doubts that she belonged to him.

What will happen when Devon marries Ashley?
Find out in Maya Banks's passionate new novel
TEMPTED BY HER INNOCENT KISS
Available March 2012 from Harlequin Desire!

Harlequin *Presents*

USA TODAY bestselling author

Carol Marinelli

begins a daring duet.

THE SECRETS
of
XANOS

*Two brothers alike in charisma and power;
separated at birth and seeking revenge…*

Nico has always felt like an outsider. He's turned his back on his parents' fortune to become one of Xanos's most powerful exports and nothing will stand in his way—until he stumbles upon a virgin bride….

Zander took his chances on the streets rather than spending another moment under his cruel father's roof. Now he is unrivaled in business—and the bedroom! He wants the best people around him, and Charlotte is the best PA! Can he tempt her over to the dark side…?

A SHAMEFUL CONSEQUENCE
Available in March

AN INDECENT PROPOSITION
Available in April

www.Harlequin.com

HP13053